BLUE BAMBOO:
TALES BY
DAZAI OSAMU

Blue Bamboo: Tales by Dazai Osamu

Translated and with
an introduction by
Ralph F. McCarthy

Kurodahan Press

2012

Blue Bamboo: Tales by Dazai Osamu
Translated by Ralph F. McCarthy

FG-JP0040A2
ISBN: 978-4-902075-58-8

KURODAHAN.COM

Contents

TRANSLATOR'S INTRODUCTION

Scholars and fans often divide the career of Dazai Osamu (1909–1948) into three periods—early, middle, and late. The early and late periods tend to get all the attention, but in my lonely opinion Dazai was at his best in the middle period, which corresponds roughly to the years of the Pacific War. All the stories in this collection, with the exception of the early "Romanesque," were written during that time.

These translations were first published by Kodansha International in 1993, as *Blue Bamboo: Tales of Fantasy and Romance*, but soon went out of print. Rereading the stories nearly twenty years later, I found that I still loved them but that the translations needed a lot of work. I think I've improved them considerably, and I'm grateful to Kurodahan Press for the opportunity to present these somewhat spiffed-up versions.

A few notes on the individual stories:

On Love and Beauty
(愛と美について / *Ai to bi ni tsuite*) May 1939

Please don't be deterred by the rather incomprehensible lecture on mathematics with which the youngest son opens the story-within-the-story—things sail along quite smoothly once he finally shuts up. I find myself wishing that Dazai had written dozens of stories featuring this quirky family and their favorite pastime, but in fact he left only one sequel—the last story in this collection, "Lanterns of Romance."

The Chrysanthemum Spirit
(清貧譚 / *Seihintan*) January 1941

Dazai's title, literally translated, would be something like "A Tale of Honest Poverty." The story is based loosely on a vignette from a voluminous collection of Chinese folklore and ghost stories entitled *Liao Chai Chih I*, compiled by P'u Sung-ling in the seventeenth century and partially translated by Herbert A. Giles as *Strange Tales from a Chinese Studio*. Dazai places the action in Edo (which is, of course, the old name for Tokyo) and invents the moral conflict reflected in the title he chose. I have deleted from the translation the opening paragraph, in which Dazai introduces the work. Here it is:

> The following is based on a tale from the *Liao Chai Chih I*. The original consists of a mere 1,834 Chinese characters, which would fill only about four and a half sheets of the standard manuscript paper we use in Japan. An extraordinarily short little piece, but reading it triggers such a flood of images in the mind that one experiences as complete a sense of satisfaction as might be garnered from most stories of thirty pages or more, and what I'd like to do is to set down the various meanderings of the imagination that occurred to me as I read it. It might be argued that in doing

so I'm straying from the proper path as a writer, but since I consider the *Liao Chai Chih I* to be more a sort of source-book of folklore than a classic of literature, I don't think it would be such a terrible sin for a twentieth-century author to make use of his unruly daydreams and impressions to fashion a tale based essentially on one of these old stories and present it to the reader as an original work. There is a lot of talk these days about a "new order," but my own personal new order would appear to be nothing more nor less than the exhumation of romanticism.

The Mermaid and the Samurai

(人魚の海 / *Ningyo no umi*) October 1944

This is one of the twelve retellings of stories by Ihara Saikaku (1642-1693) that Dazai published during World War II. Dazai's title literally means "The Sea of Mermaids." While the story follows the basic outline of Saikaku's "The Sea of Life-taking Mermaids" (which is a mere three or four pages in length), Dazai expands freely, adding characters and details and turning the whole thing into a near-parody of the melodramatic samurai plays and movies of his time. The following is from an introduction Dazai wrote to his collection of Saikaku tales:

> I have entitled this collection *New Tales of the Provinces* but am tempted to give it the subtitle *My Saikaku*. Whatever it is, it is not a modern translation of Saikaku. Modern translations of classics are, generally speaking, pointless endeavors—certainly nothing that anyone who calls himself an author should undertake. About three years ago I published a short story called "A Tale of Honest Poverty," which was based on a piece from the *Liao Chai Chih I* but greatly embellished with my own vagrant musings, and I have used the same method for the present collection.

Blue Bamboo

(竹青 / *Chikusei*) April 1945

This, too, is a very loose retelling of a story in *Liao Chai Chih I* (included in Giles's translation under the title "The Man Who Was Changed into a Crow"). Dazai preserves the basic situation and little else: the moral dilemma and its resolution are entirely of his own invention, and the countless references to Chinese classics—most of which would have been familiar to Japanese readers in 1945—are nowhere to be found in the original. Dazai appended an "author's note," in which he tells us: "This is an original work. I wrote it in the hope that it would be read by the people of China. It is to be translated into Chinese."

"Blue Bamboo" was, in fact, published in that language (in the Japanese Imperial Government-sponsored journal *Greater East Asian Literature*) even before it was published in Japanese.

Alt Heidelberg

(老ハイデルベルヒ / *Aruto Haideruberuhi*) March 1940

This story is perhaps the odd man out here, in that it's a blatantly autobiographical first-person narrative, but we think it makes a nice companion piece.

Romanesque

(ロマネスク / *Romanesuku*) November 1934

"Romanesque" was included in Dazai's first collection of stories, *The Twilight Years*. He often described it as his "debut work" and always seemed to remain quite fond of it, although some readers may be inclined to agree with this comment from "On *The Twilight Years*," an essay he wrote in 1938: "'Romanesque,' for example, is full of comical absurdities, but it's a bit out of control, so I can't really recommend it all that highly."

Lanterns of Romance

(ロマン燈籠/ *Roman dōrō*) December 1940–June 1941

Dazai's well-documented reverence of Hans Christian Andersen is indicated here by his letting our old friend, the youngest son, plagiarize extended passages from "The Snow Queen" almost verbatim.

At the beginning of "Lanterns of Romance," Dazai reproduces (with only a few very minor changes) the first three or four pages of "On Love and Beauty," and I have had to do some cutting and patching here—deleting even a bit more than merely the redundant material. To ease my conscience, and because it seems a fitting way to end this perhaps superfluous introduction, allow me to present the bulk of my additional deletion here. Dazai is referring to "On Love and Beauty" in this passage:

Being an unpopular writer, I didn't manage to get the story published immediately in a magazine, and for a long time it remained in the bottom of my desk drawer. Since I also had three or four other unpublished works laid aside—hidden treasures, if you will—in early spring of the year before last I suddenly threw them all together for publication in a single volume. Even now I retain a certain fondness for that collection, meager as it is. All the works are naive, sentimental little offerings, but they nonetheless gave me great pleasure to write and were conceived without the least trace of ambition or ulterior design. So-called *tours de force* tend somehow to be awkward affairs that, upon rereading, can leave even the author with an unpleasant taste in his mouth, but this is a defect that short, carefree little pieces do not share. As usual, that collection of stories didn't sell very well, but I wasn't particularly disappointed. At times I even think it's a good thing it didn't sell. Though I feel affection for the stories, I don't consider

DAZAI OSAMU

them to be of the highest quality in terms of content. They are all, in a sense, sloppy works that simply aren't capable of standing up to a stern, objective reading. But an author's affection doesn't always correspond to his objective judgment, and I sometimes find myself stealthily spreading that treacly collection of stories out on my desk and rereading them. Of all the tales in the collection, the most frivolous, and the one that the author loves most dearly, is the very one I refer to above, the one inspired by those five brothers and sisters. . . .

ON LOVE AND BEAUTY

There were five brothers and sisters, and all of them loved romances.

The eldest son was twenty-eight and a Bachelor of Laws. He tended to come across as arrogant and standoffish, but this was only a forbidding mask to disguise his own vulnerability; he was in fact a fragile and very gentle person. Even as he complained, whenever the brothers and sisters went to the movies, that the samurai film they were watching was rubbish, or silly, he was always the first to burst into tears, overwhelmed by the main character's inner conflict between duty and heart. Always. On emerging from the movie theater, however, he'd be wearing a petulant sort of scowl, and all the way home he'd refuse to utter a single word.

He often professed, without the least hesitation, that he'd never told a lie in his life. Doubtful as that may be, it is true that he had a certain virtuous, irreproachable side to his character. His marks in school had not been very good, and after graduation he hadn't sought employment but had devoted himself instead to looking after the family. He was currently involved in research on Ibsen. Recently, upon rereading *A Doll's House*, he had made a major discovery and worked himself into quite a lather: Nora was in love. She was in love with the doctor, Rank. That was his discovery. He called the brothers and sisters

3

together, pointed out the relevant passage, and attempted
to explain it to them in a commanding bellow, but all in
vain. Far from sharing his excitement, the brothers and
sisters merely cocked their heads, grinning and murmuring "H'mm," or "I wonder." They were not inclined to
take their eldest brother very seriously, and at times even
seemed to regard him as somewhat comical.

The elder daughter, who was twenty-five and still
unwed, worked at the Railways Ministry. She boasted a
rather good command of French. She was tall and very
thin, with a long, narrow face, and her younger siblings
sometimes referred to her as "The Horse." Her hair was
cut short, and she wore round glasses with black frames.
Warm and gregarious by nature, she made friends easily
and became thoroughly attached to them, only to be abandoned in due course. This was, in fact, her hobby; secretly
she took pleasure in the heartache and melancholia such
rejections afforded her. Once, however, when she fell hard
for a young official in her department and was, as usual,
cast aside, her devastation was quite real, and because the
situation at work was as awkward as it was disheartening,
she thought it best to plead lung problems. After lying in
bed for a week with bandages wrapped around her neck,
coughing like mad, she was finally taken to see a specialist,
who studied her X-rays and congratulated her on having as
healthy a set of lungs as he'd ever seen.

Her real love, in any case, was literature. She read a
tremendous amount, and her tastes knew no historical
or geographical bounds. She was also stealthily writing
something of her own, a treasure that she kept hidden in
the right-hand drawer of her bookcase. Placed neatly atop
the manuscript was a note that read: "To be made public

two years after my death." The "two years" was amended occasionally to read "ten years" or "two months" or even, at times, "one hundred years."

The second son was twenty-three. He was a snob. Though enrolled in medical school at the Imperial University, he rarely attended classes, being frail of constitution and frequently ill. He had a face that was almost startlingly lovely. And he was a miser. When the eldest son proudly brought home a ridiculous, worn-out old tennis racket that had supposedly been used by Montaigne and that he bragged of having purchased, after much haggling, for fifty yen, the second son, overwhelmed by the attempt to conceal his righteous indignation, came down with a bad fever that eventually did damage to his kidneys.

He had a tendency to look down on others. Whenever someone ventured an opinion on any topic he would respond with a scornful, uncanny laugh, a grating cackle like the call of some sort of goblin crow. His one and only idol was Goethe, although there was something suspicious about his admiration of the man: he seemed to respect the Master not so much for his pure, poetic spirit as for the lofty social status he enjoyed. But the fact remains that whenever the brothers and sisters held competitions in impromptu verse, the second son always came out on top. He was a natural poet. Precisely because he was such a snob, he had a well-defined, objective grasp of human passion, and if he'd put his mind to it he might even have become an acclaimed writer. A slightly lame sixteen-year-old maid who worked for the family was hopelessly in love with him.

The younger daughter was twenty. She was a narcissist. When a certain newspaper held a campaign to find Miss

Japan, she was so tormented by the question of whether or not to nominate herself that she tossed and turned in bed for three consecutive nights, suppressing an urge to scream and tear at her hair. She found relief only when it came to her attention that she was too short to qualify for the competition anyway, and promptly erased the whole thing from her mind. Of all the brothers and sisters, she alone was extraordinarily petite, standing only four feet, seven inches tall. But by no means was she unattractive. She was, in fact, quite an eyeful. Late at night, she would sit in front of a mirror in the nude, practicing coy smiles, or spreading lotion on her shapely white legs, then softly kissing her fingertips and closing her eyes as if enraptured. Once, when a pimple the size of a pinprick appeared on the tip of her nose, she grew so depressed that she almost committed suicide.

There was a distinctive character to the younger daughter's choice of reading material. She would go to used book stores to search out such works of the early Meiji era as *Chance Encounters with Beautiful Women* and *Inspirational Tales of Leadership*. These she would bring home and pore over, chuckling to herself as she read. She enjoyed contemporary foreign works in translation, and she also managed somehow to accumulate a great number of obscure little coterie magazines, which she would read from cover to cover, muttering "How amusing!" or "Clever, very clever!" But her real favorite—though she kept this to herself—was the great romantic Izumi Kyōka.

The youngest son was seventeen. He had just matriculated at Tokyo First Higher School, where he was enrolled in the science department. Upon entering higher school, his personality had undergone a sudden transformation.

ON LOVE AND BEAUTY

This was a source of great hilarity for the elder brothers and sisters, but the youngest son took his newfound sophistication quite seriously indeed. When a minor dispute of any sort arose in the household, he would inevitably stick his nose into the matter and, though no one was asking him to, pronounce his carefully considered judgment. The entire family was appalled by this and tended to give him a wide berth these days, but the elder daughter, who could not bear to see him sulking and pouting, had written a poem to console him in his lonely exile:

> *Ah, the sadness of*
> *having become a grownup,*
> *mature in every way,*
> *and being the only one*
> *who knows it.*

His face resembled that of a bear cub, and the elder brothers and sisters in fact found him adorable and had always tended to pamper him. As a result of this treatment, he was a bit scatterbrained. He loved detective stories and from time to time, alone in his room, experimented with disguises. He'd recently bought a dual-language edition of Conan Doyle stories, purportedly for the purpose of studying English, but in fact he was reading only the Japanese translation. He quietly suffered the tragic conviction that of all the brothers and sisters, he alone worried about their mother sufficiently.

The father had died some five years before, but there was no threat to their standard of living. Which is to say that they were a family of some substance. Occasionally they were all overcome with a suffocating sense of boredom, and such was the case on this particular day. It was a dark and cloudy Sunday. Summer was on its way, but first the gloomy rainy season must be endured. They'd all gathered in the drawing room, where the mother was dispensing apple juice to her five children. The youngest son's cup was considerably larger than everyone else's.

It was customary in this household for the brothers and sisters to relieve bouts of boredom by taking turns spinning out a collective story. The mother too sometimes joined in.

"Any ideas?" The eldest son swept a pompous gaze over the assemblage. "I'd like today's protagonist to be a bit eccentric, perhaps."

"Let's make him an elderly man." The younger daughter struck a hopelessly affected pose—elbow on table, chin on palm, forefinger raised to rest against cheek. "I gave this a lot of thought last night"—it had, in fact, just occurred to her at that moment—"and I realized that elderly men comprise the most romantic category of human beings. An old woman won't do at all. It has to be a man. An elderly man can be merely sitting on a veranda, and that's all it takes, it's already romantic. Ahh . . ."

"An old man, eh?" The eldest son pretended to think it over for a moment. "All right, so be it. Let's make it a nice story, though, full of sweetness and light. 'The Return of Gulliver' last time was a bit too dark. I mean . . . I've been rereading Brand recently, and I have to admit it makes my shoulders stiff. It's just too harrowing." A rare confession.

"I'll go first!" The youngest son nominated himself in a shrill voice without bothering to pause and arrange his thoughts. He gulped down his apple juice. And then, slowly and deliberately, he began setting forth his ideas.

"I, uh . . . I . . . Allow me to explain how I see it." The others smiled ruefully at his attempt to sound mature, and the second son produced his famous jeering cackle, but the youngest forged ahead.

"I think this elderly gentleman must be a great mathematician. Yes, I'm sure of it. A great and renowned mathematician. A Doctor of Mathematics, naturally, and a world-class scholar. Mathematics is changing drastically these days, as I'm sure you're all well aware. It's going through a transitional period. This has been underway for the past ten years or so—since about 1920, to be more precise, or just after the end of the World War."

It was painfully obvious that he was parroting, word for word, a lecture he'd attended at school the day before.

"If one looks back on the history of mathematics, one can see how the science has evolved in concert with the times. The first stage in this process came with the discovery of differential and integral calculus. That spawned what in broad terms we might call modern mathematics, as opposed to the traditional Greek variety. New territory had been opened, and directly afterward we had a period of, not refinement, strictly speaking, but expansion. That was the mathematics of the eighteenth century. As we move into the nineteenth century we find, sure enough, another rash of new ideas, and this too was a time of sudden change. To choose one representative figure, we might mention Gauss, for example. That's G, a, u, double-s. But if we define a transitional period as a time during which continual, rapid change takes place, then the present is, indeed, a transitional period to end all transitional periods."

9

This was of no use whatsoever—least of all as a story. The youngest son was nonetheless positively triumphant, convinced that he was beginning to hit his stride.

"Things have become extremely complicated. We are now awash in a deluge of theorems, and mathematics as we know it has reached a dead end. It has been reduced to a science of mere rote memorization. And the one man who at this crucial juncture has dared to stand up and proclaim freedom for mathematics is none other than our elderly professor. He's a great man. Had he become a detective, he undoubtedly would have solved even the most difficult and bizarre case after nothing more than a quick stroll through the scene of the crime. That's how brilliant he is. At any rate, as Cantor himself has put it,"—here we go again—"freedom is the very essence of mathematics. This is certainly true.

"Our word for 'freedom'—*jiyūsei*—was coined as a translation of the German *Freiheit*. But it's said that the Japanese word was originally used in a strictly political sense and may not be an exact equivalent. *Freiheit* is a simple concept that means 'not enslaved,' 'not subject to restraint.' Examples of things that are not *frei* are to be found in any number of familiar places . . . so many, in fact, that it's difficult to choose a single illustration. But take our telephone number, for example, which, as you all know, is four eight two three. How do we write it? With a comma between the first and second integers. Four comma eight two three. Now, if we were to write it with a slash, as they do in Paris—four eight slash two three—one could see the logic, but this custom of separating each group of three digits with a comma is nothing less than a form of slavery. Our elderly professor is making every effort to smash such corrupt conventions. He is a great man. Poincaré tells us that the only thing worthy of our love is truth, and I heartily agree. To grasp the truth in a concise and direct manner is the highest of human endeavors. There is nothing superior to it."

So, what about the story? The other brothers and sisters were by now exchanging disconcerted looks, but the youngest son remained oblivious to them as he plowed ahead with his wobbly thesis.

"To enter the realm of empty academic theory is to run the risk of digressing from the point, but if I might ask you to bear with me for a moment, it so happens that I am currently engaged in the study of mathematical analysis, and since it is rather fresh in my mind, I should like to present a certain problem inherent in this field as an example of what I'm trying to say. These days it has become customary for treatments of mathematical analysis to begin with a discussion of the theory of sets—a questionable tendency in and of itself. Tradition, it would seem, can inspire in people an almost religious faith, and this sort of blind dogmatism has even begun to infiltrate the world of mathematics. It must be driven out at all costs. And that is precisely what our elderly professor has taken it upon himself to do—to rise to the battle against tradition."

The youngest son was growing noticeably excited. Everyone else was bored to tears, but he had roused himself to a righteous fervor worthy of his elderly professor.

"Let's examine the case of absolute convergence. In the past, 'absolute convergence' meant that a sum was conditionally constant irrespective of order or sequence—the operative word being 'conditionally.' What it means nowadays, on the other hand, is simply that progression series of absolute value must converge. It's said that if progression series converge and progression series of absolute value do not converge, one can change the order of the terms to make them tend to an arbitrary limit, so it turns out that . . . that they converge anyway, so . . . so it's all right." Suddenly he was losing his grasp on the subject. He felt terribly alone. He thought of the textbook by Professor Takagi sitting on the desk in his room, but he could hardly stop here and go get it. Everything was explained clearly in the book. He was on the verge of tears. His voice faltered, his breast was trembling, and in a tone so shrill it resembled a shriek he said: "*In short . . .*"

The brothers and sisters all sat with bowed heads, giggling to themselves.

"In short," he said again, suppressing a sob, "the problem with tradition is that it can cause even an error of great magnitude to go unnoticed, but there are a lot of problematic little details involved that we don't have time to go into here. In any case, I would like to express my fervent wish for the publication of an introduction to mathematical analysis that has a freer point of view and is more accessible to the layman."

And here the youngest son's part of the story ended. What a mess. A chill had even fallen over the room. There was simply no way to continue the story, nothing to graft onto. Everyone seemed lost in morbid contemplation. The elder daughter, however, being the compassionate person she was, wanted to come to her youngest sibling's aid. She stifled a final giggle, composed herself, and began to speak in a quiet voice.

"As the preceding discussion has amply demonstrated, our elderly professor is a man of lofty character. A lofty character is always shadowed by adversity. This is a rule with no exceptions. The old professor doesn't fit in. Forever regarded as strange or eccentric by his neighbors, he can't help but feel miserably lonely at times, and on this particular night he is, as usual, alone, as he picks up his walking stick and heads for Shinjuku.

"Our story takes place in summer. Great crowds of people throng the streets of Shinjuku. The professor presents a heartrending sight in his old, wrinkled, cotton *yukata*, with the sash tied high above his waist and the loose ends dangling down almost to his heels, like the tail of a rat. What makes things worse is that, although the professor is a man who perspires a great deal, he has forgotten his handkerchief. At first he wipes his brow with the palm of his hand, but this method proves no match for such a prodigious amount of sweat. It gushes from his forehead like water overflowing a mountain pool, streaming down his nose and temples, washing over the entire surface of his face, and dripping from his chin to his chest, and he feels perfectly wretched, as if he's had a jug of sticky camellia oil dumped over his head. He finally begins to use the sleeves of his yukata, swiftly passing one sleeve over his face, walking a few steps, then surreptitiously doing the same with the other sleeve, and before long both sleeves are drenched. The professor is by nature indifferent to appearances, but this flood of perspiration is just too much for him, and at last he decides to take refuge in a beer hall.

"Inside, the air being pushed around by the fans is warm and damp, but at least his perspiration subsides somewhat. The radio in the beer hall is blaring a lecture on current affairs, and suddenly the professor takes notice of the voice delivering the lecture. It's a voice he's heard before. *It sounds like that weasel*, he thinks, and sure enough, when the lecture ends, the announcer comes on to pronounce the name of 'that weasel,' attaching the honorific title 'His Excellency.' The professor wishes he could wash out his ears. The weasel is a man who studied alongside the professor throughout higher school and university—a calculating schemer who climbed to a lofty position in the Ministry of Education. Now and then the professor and the weasel have occasion to come face to face at class reunions or academic conferences, and each time they meet, the weasel heaps gratuitous derision upon him. He delivers a series of boorish, banal jibes, and although nothing he says is the least bit funny, the members of his entourage laugh uproariously at every word, all but slapping their knees. On one such occasion the professor kicked his chair back and rose to his feet in a rage but unfortunately stepped on an orange he'd dropped earlier, squishing it and allowing a startled, feeble shriek to escape his lips. 'Eek!' he cried, at which the entire company exploded with laughter. Thus the professor's righteous anger ended in a sad and pitiful farce. But he is not about to give up. He's determined to punch that weasel in the nose one day.

"Hearing his loathsome, grating voice on the radio has put the professor in a most unpleasant mood, and he gulps down a beer. Never having been one to hold his liquor very well, he grows tipsy almost at once. A young girl selling fortunes enters the beer hall. The professor calls her over and in a soft, familiar tone of voice says: 'How old are you, dear? Thirteen? You don't say. That means that in another five years . . . no, four years . . . no, no, in another three years, you can get married. Now listen carefully. How much is thirteen plus three? H'mm?' And so on. Even a respected professor of mathematics can behave rather inappropriately when drunk. Now, however, having been somewhat overly persistent in teasing the girl, he realizes he has little choice but to buy one of her fortunes. The professor is not a superstitious man, but tonight, partially because of the radio broadcast, he feels somewhat vulnerable and has a sudden urge to consult the fortune as to what will become of his research, and where his destiny will lead him. When one's life begins to unravel, one is tempted, sadly enough, to cling to the thread of prophecy.

"The fortune is of the invisible ink variety. The professor heats the paper with the flame of a match, opening his bleary eyes wide in an attempt to focus on the words as they appear. At first he's uncertain what he's seeing—it merely looks like some sort of design—but gradually the lines resolve into clear-cut characters written in a flowing, old-fashioned style:

JUST AS YOU WISH

"Seeing this, the professor beams. Well, no, 'beams' is hardly the word. Our noble professor erupts with a vulgar-sounding chuckle—'Er, her, her, her'—then thrusts out his chin and looks about at the other drunken customers. None of them take any particular notice of the professor, but that doesn't stop him from nodding to each of them and producing a series of silly laughs—'Ha, ha. Just as you wish! Hee, hee, hee. Excuse me. Ho, ho!'—as he strolls serenely out of the beer hall, his self-confidence thoroughly restored.

"Outside, a slow-moving river of people flows over the street. It's quite a crush. People jostling and shoving, all of them dripping with sweat but trying to look composed and indifferent as they shuffle along. They're walking with no goal or destination in mind, to be sure, but precisely

15

because their daily lives are so dreary they are harboring, all of them, some faint flicker of hope that compels them to stroll through the Shinjuku night with looks of cool composure on their faces. Walk up and down those streets all you like, not a single good thing will come of it. This much is certain. But happiness is being able to hope, however faintly, for happiness. So, at least, we must believe if we are to live in the world of today. Discharged from the beer hall's revolving door, the professor totters and dives into the city's sad current of migrant souls and is at once jostled and swept downstream, floundering and flailing as if he were drowning. Tonight, however, of all the members of this vast throng, the professor is quite possibly the one with the greatest confidence. The odds of his obtaining happiness are better than anyone else's. Recalling his good fortune from time to time as he walks along, he smiles or nods to himself, or raises his eyebrows to give his expression a grave and dignified aspect, or makes inept and rather uncouth attempts at whistling.

"Then, suddenly, he collides head-on with a young student. This, however, is only to be expected. In a crowd this size, it's natural that one will bump into someone else occasionally. Nothing comes of the encounter; the student merely walks on. But a short while later the professor collides with a beautiful young lady. Nothing comes of this either, though: she merely continues along the street. It is not yet time for happiness to arrive. The new development is to come from behind him. Someone taps the professor lightly on the back. This time it's no accident."

The elder daughter stopped there. She'd been speaking all this time with downcast eyes. Now she snatched off her glasses and began vigorously polishing the lenses with her handkerchief—something she always did when self-conscious.

The second son continued.

"I'm afraid I'm not very good at doing descriptive passages. Or, rather, it's not that I'm not good at it, it's just that it seems like too much trouble today. So I'll keep this brief and to the point." Such cheek.

"The professor turns to see a plump woman of about forty. She's holding a small dog with a remarkably ugly face. The two of them have the following conversation.

"'Happy?' she says.

"'Sure, I'm happy. Since you've been gone, everything's fine. Everything's, well, just as I wish.'

"'H'mph. I suppose you've got yourself some young thing?'

"'Something wrong with that?'

"'Yes, there is something wrong with that. Didn't you promise me that if I only gave up dogs I could return to you any time I pleased?'

"'That's not likely to happen, though, is it? God, this one's a real horror. Just horrible. It looks like a creature that eats larvae or something. What a monstrosity. Ugh. It's nauseating.'

"'You don't have to go all pale in the face for my benefit. Isn't that right, Pro? Is the bad man making fun of you? Bark at him. Go on. Woof! Woof!'

"'Stop that. You're as contrary as ever, aren't you. You know, just talking to you sends chills down my spine.

17

"Pro"? What the hell is that? Can't you come up with a name with a bit more class? Idiot.'

"'What's wrong with "Pro"? It's short for "Professor." I named him in honor of you. Isn't he sweet?'

"'I can't stand this.'

"'My! You still perspire as much as ever, don't you? Goodness! Don't wipe it off with your sleeve. How do you think that looks? Don't you have a handkerchief? Your new wife must be an awfully careless person. I never once forgot to see that you had three handkerchiefs and a fan whenever you went out in summer.'

"'I won't have you finding fault with my hallowed home. It's most unpleasant.'

"'Well, excuse me. Here. Take this handkerchief.'

"'Thanks. I'll just borrow it for the time being.'

"'You've become a complete stranger, haven't you?'

"'When two people separate, they become strangers. That's just the way it . . . Wait . . . This handkerchief . . . Sure enough, it has the same old . . . No. No, it smells of dogs.'

"'What a thing to say. The fragrance brings back memories, doesn't it?'

"'Don't be stupid. You know what your problem is? Ill breeding.'

"'Me? What about yourself? Do you insist on your new wife babying you too? You mustn't, you know, at your age. How do you think it looks? She'll grow to hate you. Having her put your socks on you while you're still in bed, and—'

18

"'I told you I won't have you finding fault with my hallowed home. Listen, I'm happy now. Everything's going splendidly.'

"'And do you still have soup in the morning? With one raw egg? Or two?'

"'Two. Sometimes three. I have more of everything now than I did with you. I'll tell you, when I look back, I get the feeling there can't be many women in this world with a tongue as sharp as yours. Why did you have to yell at me so much? I felt like an unwanted guest in my own home. Dining ill and supping worse. I haven't forgotten that. I was working on some very important research in those days, you know. You didn't understand that at all. Nagging me from morning to night about the buttons on my vest, or my cigarette butts . . . Thanks to you my research, and everything else in my life, was a shambles. As soon as I split up with you, I ripped every button off my vest and started throwing all my cigarette butts into coffee cups. That was a wonderful feeling. Absolutely exhilarating. I laughed so hard, all by myself, that tears came to my eyes. But the more I thought about it, the more I realized how I'd suffered at your hands. Afterwards, I just grew angrier and angrier. Even now, I'm plenty angry. You don't have any idea how to treat a person.'

"'I'm sorry. I was young. Forgive me. I . . . I . . . Now I understand. The dogs were never really the problem, were they?'

"'There you go, wringing out the tears again. That always was your way. Well, it won't work anymore. Right now, for me, everything is just as I wish. See? You want to have a cup of tea somewhere?'

19

"'I can't. I . . . Now I understand perfectly. You and I have become strangers, haven't we? No, we always were strangers. Our hearts were in different worlds, a thousand miles, a million miles apart. If we were together, we'd only be miserable, both of us. I want to make a clean break with you now. I . . . You see, I'm going to have a hallowed home of my own soon.'

"'Oh? You found a good prospect?'

"'It'll be fine. He's . . . He works in a factory. He's the foreman. I understand that if it weren't for him, the machines in the factory wouldn't run at all. He's a big man . . . A mountain of a man. Solid as a rock.'

"'Not like me, eh?'

"'No. He's not a scholar. He doesn't do research or anything. But he's awfully good at what he does.'

"'I'm sure you'll be very happy. Goodbye, then. I'll just borrow this handkerchief for now.'

"'Goodbye. Ah! Your sash is coming undone. Here, I'll tie it for you. Really, there's no end to looking after you, is there? Give my regards to your wife.'

"'Sure. If I think of it.'"

The second brother fell silent, then let out a self-deprecating cackle. If his observations seemed strangely sophisticated for one of his youth, this was nothing new.

"I already know how it ends." The younger daughter smugly continued. "Here's what happens, I'm quite sure. After the professor parts with the woman, there's a sudden downpour. No wonder it's been so humid. The people walking the streets scatter in every direction, like a batch of newborn spiders. It's like magic, the way they disappear, and the streets of Shinjuku, which were so crowded only moments before, are now silent and empty of everything but the rain splattering in silver explosions on the pavement. The professor takes refuge under the eaves of a flower shop, hunching his shoulders and shrinking into a crouch. From time to time he pulls out the handkerchief and gazes at it for a moment, then hastily stuffs it back into his sleeve.

"It occurs to him to buy some flowers. If he does that and brings them back to his wife, who's waiting at home, she's sure to be delighted. Never before in the professor's life has he purchased flowers. He's not quite himself today. The radio, the fortune, the ex-wife, the handkerchief—a lot has transpired. Coming to a momentous resolve, he dashes into the flower shop and, though he's terribly flustered and embarrassed and sweating profusely, somehow summons the courage to buy three large, long-stemmed roses. He's shocked at how expensive they are. Outside the flower shop, he grabs a taxi and heads straight for home.

"The lantern glows brightly over the front door of his house on the outskirts of town. Home, sweet home. A refuge of warmth and comfort, the one place where everything goes splendidly. As he opens the door, he calls out in a loud voice: 'I'm home!' He's in high spirits. It's silent inside, but that doesn't stop him. Bearing the flowers like a torch, he marches through the house and enters his study.

"'I'm home. Got caught in the rain—what an ordeal! How do you like these? I'm told everything will turn out just as I wish.'

"He's speaking to a photograph that sits atop his desk. It's a photo of the woman with whom he has just made a

21

clean break. But, no, not as she is now. It's a photo taken a decade ago. She wears a beautiful smile."

Narcissus struck her affected pose again, chin on hand, forefinger against cheek, and gazed about the room as if to say: "Nothing to it."

"Yes. Well," the eldest son began with a pedantic air. "I suppose that more or less wraps things up. However . . ." As the eldest, he had his dignity to maintain. Compared to the other brothers and sisters, he had not been blessed with a very rich imagination and was incompetent at telling stories. He simply lacked talent in that direction. But to be excluded by the others for such a reason would have been unbearable for him. He therefore tended to add something superfluous to the end of each story. "However, you've all left out an essential point in the narrative. I refer to the professor's physical appearance." It was the best he could do.

"The description of physical appearance is extremely important in a work of fiction. By describing what a character looks like, you bring him alive and remind people of someone close to them, thereby lending intimacy to the tale and involving the audience, so that they cease to be mere passive observers. The way I see it, the elderly professor is a small man—five feet, two inches tall and less than a hundred and ten pounds. As for his face, it is round, with a high, broad, deeply furrowed forehead, thin eyebrows, a small nose, a wide, firm mouth, a white, bushy beard, and silver-rimmed spectacles." This was nothing less than a description of the eldest son's revered Ibsen. Such was the trivial nature of his powers of imagination. He appeared to have succeeded, as usual, in adding something that amounted to almost nothing.

With this, at any rate, the story ended, and no sooner had it done so than boredom returned with a vengeance; the brothers and sisters all fell victim to the oppressive sense of bleakness that comes after a small bit of stimulation. An ugly mood hung over the room, stifling small talk; it was as if a single word from any of them might have resulted in blows.

The mother, who'd sat apart from the others throughout, smiling dreamily as her five children revealed their characters one by one in the way they advanced the story, now got quietly to her feet and went to the paper screen door. She slid it open, then gasped and said: "Goodness! There's a strange old man in a frock coat standing at the gate, staring in."

All five of the brothers and sisters jumped to their feet, aghast.

Their mother doubled over laughing.

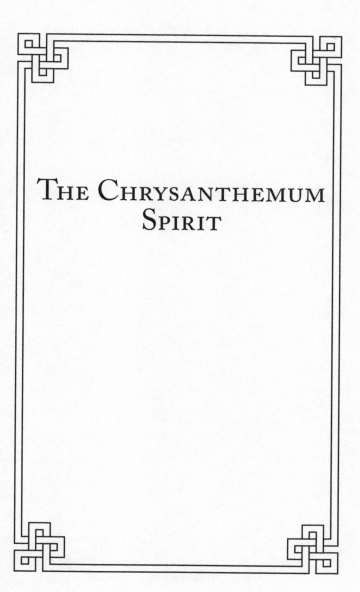

THE CHRYSANTHEMUM SPIRIT

nce upon a time, in Mukōjima in Edo, there lived a man with the rather uninteresting name of Mayama Sainosuke. Sainosuke was very poor and still a bachelor at the age of thirty-two. Chrysanthemums were the great love of his life. If told of an excellent strain of chrysanthemum seedlings being grown in some corner of the land, he would go to the most absurd lengths to search them out and purchase a few for his own garden. It's said that he'd undertake such a mission though it meant a journey of a thousand leagues, which ought to give you some idea of just how far gone he was.

One year in early autumn Sainosuke received word of an extraordinary variety of mums in the town of Numazu in Izu, and no sooner had he heard the news than he changed into his traveling gear and set out with a strange gleam in his eye. He crossed the mountains of Hakone, swept into Numazu, and tramped through the streets until he located and acquired a couple of truly splendid seedlings. After carefully wrapping these treasures in oilpaper, he smiled smugly to himself and headed for home.

As he was crossing back over the mountains of Hakone, with the city of Odawara just coming into view below, Sainosuke became aware of the clip-clop of a horse's hooves on the road behind him. Euphoric over the purchase of his precious mums, he thought nothing of this at

27

first, but when the animal continued to follow him at the same distance, neither drawing nearer nor falling behind, clopping along with the same leisurely rhythm for five, eight, ten miles, he began to wonder about it, and finally he turned to look back. Not more than twenty paces behind him was an emaciated old horse, upon which sat a youth with strikingly handsome features. He flashed a smile, and Sainosuke, not wanting to appear impolite, returned the smile and stopped to wait for him. The youth rode up, dismounted, and said: "Lovely day, isn't it?"

"It is a lovely day," Sainosuke agreed.

And with that they continued walking along side by side, the youth leading his horse by the reins. Looking his companion over, Sainosuke could see that, though clearly not of samurai stock, the lad possessed a certain elegance of bearing; he was neatly dressed and had an easy, confident way about him.

"Headed for Edo?" the youth asked in a disarmingly familiar manner, and Sainosuke responded in kind: "Yep. Going back home."

"Oh, you live there, then. And where have you been to?"

Small talk between travelers is always the same. In the course of exchanging the usual information, Sainosuke divulged the purpose of his trip to Numazu, and at the mention of chrysanthemums the young man's eyes lit up.

"You don't say! It's always a pleasure to meet someone who loves mums. I know a thing or two about them myself, you see. I must say, though, that it's not so much the quality of the seedlings as how you care for them." He was beginning to describe his own method of cultivation when Sainosuke interrupted him excitedly.

"Well, I can't agree with you there!" Chrysanthemum fanatic that he was, the topic was one that stimulated his strongest passions. "If you ask me, it's absolutely vital to have the best seedlings. Let me give you an example," he said, and proceeded to hold forth at some length, drawing upon the extensive knowledge he'd acquired over the years. The youth didn't contest Sainosuke's opinions in so many words, but his occasional muttered interjections of "Oh?" and "H'mm" and so on not only suggested that he disagreed but somehow seemed to hint at an uncommon depth of experience. The more zealously Sainosuke preached, the less confident he felt of himself, and finally, in a voice that was nearly a sob, he said: "Enough! Not another word. Theory will get us nowhere. The only way to convince you I'm right would be to show you the mums in my garden."

"I suppose that's true," the youth said, nodding rather indifferently. Sainosuke, for his part, had worked himself into quite a state. He was so eager to show this young man his chrysanthemums and make him gasp in awe that he was literally trembling.

"All right, then," he said, throwing all caution to the wind. "What do you say to this: Come with me straight to my house in Edo and see my mums for yourself. One quick look, that's all I ask."

The youth laughed. "Unfortunately I'm in no position to oblige you there. As soon as we reach Edo I've got to start searching for work."

"Don't be ridiculous." Sainosuke wasn't about to take no for an answer now. "You can find a job after you've come to my house and rested up. You've simply got to see my chrysanthemums."

"I'm afraid you're putting me on the spot here." The youth was no longer smiling. He walked along for some time with his head bowed in thought, then finally looked up and said, in a rather doleful tone of voice: "Allow me to explain. My name's Tōmoto Saburō. My elder sister and I have been living alone in Numazu since our parents died. That was some years ago, but recently my sister took a sudden disliking to the place and began to insist we move to Edo. Finally we disposed of our belongings and, well, here we are, on our way to the city. It's not as if we have any prospects waiting for us there, however, and I don't mind telling you that this is far from being a carefree, lighthearted journey. It's certainly no time to be engaging in some silly argument about chrysanthemums. I shouldn't have opened my mouth at all, and wouldn't have, except that I'm partial to mums myself. If you don't mind, I'd rather just drop the subject. Please forget I ever brought it up. My sister and I have got to be moving along anyway. Perhaps we'll meet again under more favorable circumstances."

The youth nodded goodbye and was about to climb back on the horse, but Sainosuke clutched tightly at his sleeve.

"Wait a minute. If that's how it is, then all the more reason for you to come to my house. What are you so worried about? I'm a poor man myself, but not so destitute that I can't put you up for a while. Just leave everything to me. You say you're with your sister? Where is she?"

30

THE CHRYSANTHEMUM SPIRIT

Turning, Sainosuke noticed for the first time a girl in red traveling attire peeking at him from the other side of the horse. He blushed when their eyes met.

In the end, unable to rebuff his ardent appeal, the two young people agreed to be Sainosuke's guests at his humble home in Mukōjima. When they arrived and saw that the cottage Sainosuke lived in was even more dilapidated than his professions of poverty had led them to imagine, they looked at each other and sighed. Sainosuke, however, merely ushered them straight to his garden, not even pausing to change his clothes, and delivered a long and self-congratulatory presentation on his prized mums. He then showed the pair to a little shed in the rear of the garden and explained that this was where they were to stay. Cramped as the shed was, they could see that it was at least preferable to Sainosuke's ramshackle cottage, which was so filthy and filled with trash that one hesitated even to step inside.

"Well, Sis, this is a fine state of affairs," the younger Tōmoto whispered as he undid his traveling gear inside the shed. "Prisoners of a madman."

"He is a bit strange," the sister replied with a smile. "But he seems harmless enough. I'm sure we'll be comfortable here. And the garden is certainly spacious. You must plant some nice chrysanthemums for him, to show our appreciation."

"What? Don't tell me you want to stay here for any length of time?"

"Why not? I like it here," she said, her cheeks flushing slightly. The sister was just twenty or so and lovely, with a slender figure and skin as smooth and white as porcelain.

31

By the following morning, Sainosuke and Saburō were already having the first of many arguments. The lean old horse, which the youth and his sister had taken turns riding all the way from Numazu, had disappeared. They'd left it tethered to a stake in the garden the night before, but when Sainosuke went out to check on his mums first thing in the morning it had vanished, leaving a path of destruction through his flower beds. Sainosuke took one look at the trampled, gnawed, and uprooted plants and flew into a rage. He pounded on the door of the shed.

Saburō opened it at once and said: "What is it? Something wrong?"

"See for yourself. That bandy-legged horse of yours has gone and destroyed my garden. It's enough to make me want to lie down and die!"

"It is a mess, isn't it," said the youth, calmly surveying the damage. "And the horse?"

"Who cares? He's run off, I guess."

"But that's terrible."

"What are you talking about? A rickety old nag like that!"

"I beg your pardon. That happens to be an extremely clever animal. We must go and find him immediately. The devil take your silly chrysanthemums."

"What! What did you say?" Sainosuke paled. "Are you belittling my mums?"

It was then that Saburō's sister stepped out of the shed with a demure smile on her face.

"Saburō," she said, "apologize to the gentleman. That skinny horse of ours is no great loss. I may not have tethered it properly. But the thing to do now is to fix up the chrysanthemum patch. It's a perfect chance to express our gratitude for all the kindness we've been shown."

"Oh, so that's it," Saburō groaned. "You planned this, didn't you?"

He heaved a deep sigh but grudgingly began to tend to the damaged plants. Watching him, Sainosuke couldn't help but marvel: even those mums that were nearly dead from having been trampled or uprooted sprang back to life as the youth replanted them. The roots soaked up moisture from the soil in great draughts, the stems swelled, the buds grew plump and heavy, and the wilted leaves stretched out firm and erect, pulsating with vitality. Sainosuke wasn't about to let on how astonished he was, however. He was a man who'd spent his whole life growing mums, and he had his pride to maintain.

"Well, do what you can here," he said as coolly as possible, then strode into his cottage, where he climbed in bed and buried himself beneath the quilt. Soon he was back on his feet, however, peeping out at the garden through a crack in the shutters. Sure enough, all the plants Saburō tended were springing miraculously to life.

That night Saburō came smiling to the cottage.

"Sorry about this morning," he said. "But, listen, my sister and I were talking things over, and, well, if you'll pardon my saying so, you don't seem to be leading a very comfortable life here. We were thinking that if you'd lend me half your garden, I could grow some really first-rate

33

mums for you to sell in the market in Asakusa or some-where. I'd be happy to do it."

Sainosuke, whose self-esteem as a grower of chrysan-themums had been severely shaken that morning, was not in the best of moods. Seeing this as a chance to even the score, he twisted his lips in a contemptuous sneer.

"Out of the question," he said. "Of all the vulgar ideas! And here I thought you were a man of taste and breeding. I'm shocked. To even think of selling one's beloved flow-ers simply to put food on the table! It's too outrageous for words, a violation of the very spirit of chrysanthemums! To turn a noble-minded pastime into a scheme to make money is, why it's, it's what it is. I'll have noth-ing to do with it."

Sainosuke spewed out this rebuke in the gruff and gut-tural tones of a samurai issuing a challenge, and Saburō, understandably enough, took offense. His reply was rather heated.

"Using one's god-given talent to put food on the table hardly qualifies as greed, and to sneer at me and accuse me of being vulgar for wishing to do so is appallingly wrongheaded. It's arrogant and childish—the attitude of a spoiled little brat. It's true that a man shouldn't be overly covetous of riches, but to take undue pride in one's poverty is every bit as base and mean."

"When have I ever boasted of my poverty? Look, my ancestors left me with a small inheritance, and it's all I've ever needed. I want for nothing. And I'll thank you not to meddle in my affairs."

Once again their exchange had blossomed into a full-blown row.

"You're being awfully narrow-minded, you know."

"Fine. Call me narrow-minded. Call me a spoiled brat. Call me anything you like. I simply prefer to carry on as I always have, sharing the joys and sorrows of life with my mums."

"All right, all right!" Saburō shrugged and smiled ruefully. "You win. But listen: There's a small plot of bare ground behind the shed. Would you consider lending that to us for the time being?"

"You must realize by now that I'm not a man who's attached to worldly possessions. I don't imagine you'll find such a tiny plot sufficient to your needs. Half my garden remains unplanted: take all of that if you like. Do with it as you see fit. Allow me to make one thing clear, however: I will not associate with anyone who would grow mums with the intention of offering them for sale. From this day on, I want you to consider me a complete stranger."

Saburō gaped at him incredulously for a moment, then shook his head in exasperation.

"So be it," he said. "I won't refuse such a generous offer. In fact, if I might further impose upon your generosity, I noticed that you've discarded a number of old chrysanthemum seedlings behind the shed . . ."

"You needn't bother me with requests for every trifle. Take them."

And thus they parted, on the worst of terms. The next day Sainosuke divided his garden in two and erected a tall fence along the border, obstructing the view from either side. Relations between the two households were severed.

DAZAI OSAMU

As autumn advanced, all of Sainosuke's chrysanthemums burst into beautiful bloom. Satisfying as this was, he couldn't help wondering how his neighbors' flowers had fared, and finally one day his curiosity got the best of him and he decided to peek over the fence. What he saw left him agog. The other half of the garden was ablaze from end to end with the largest and most spectacular blooms Sainosuke had ever seen. And that wasn't the only surprise. The shed had been rebuilt and was now a charming and cozy little cottage. This was hardly a sight to soothe Sainosuke's soul. Not only were his own chrysanthemums no match for Saburō's, the upstart had gone and built himself an elegant little home. No doubt he'd made a small fortune selling his mums. It was an outrage! Determined to teach the youth a lesson, he scrambled over the fence, his heart wracked with an insufferable mixture of righteous indignation and envy. Close up, Saburō's mums were even more impressive. The flowers were blooming for all they were worth; each individual petal was extraordinarily long and thick and vibrating with life. Adding insult to injury was the fact that, as Sainosuke soon realized, the plants were none other than the worthless seedlings he'd discarded behind the shed. He let out a gurgle of despair, and just as he did so a voice called to him from behind.

"Welcome! We've been waiting for you to drop by."

Flustered, Sainosuke spun around to see Saburō standing there, grinning at him.

"You win!" he nearly shouted in frustration. "I know when I'm beaten, and I'm man enough to admit it too. Listen, I'm . . . I'm here to ask you to take me on as your apprentice. Everything that's passed between us . . ." He paused to unload a great sigh of relief. "It's all just water

36

under the bridge. We'll let bygones be bygones. However, I—"

"Wait. Please don't say what I think you're going to say. I'm not a man of your moral fiber. As you've probably guessed, I've been selling off the chrysanthemums little by little. Please don't look down on us for that. My sister is always fretting about what you'll think, but we're only doing what we need to do to survive. Unlike yourself, we have no inheritance to fall back on—it's either sell the mums or die of starvation. Please be so indulgent as to overlook that, and let us be friends again."

The sincerity of Saburō's plea and the sad droop of his head melted Sainosuke's heart.

"Don't be silly," he said meekly, and bowed. "I'm not worthy of your apology. I feel no enmity toward either of you. Besides, I'm the one who's asking you be my teacher. If anyone should apologize, it's me."

And so they were reconciled, at least for the time being. Sainosuke dismantled the fence in the garden, and the members of the two households resumed relations, although, to be sure, conflicts still arose now and then.

"You must have some secret to raising these mums."

"Nothing of the sort. I've already taught you everything I know. The rest is in the fingertips, but that's where it gets a bit mysterious. I simply seem to have a certain touch, and since it's something I'm not really conscious of, I can't very well teach it to you in words. It's a genius of sorts, I suppose."

"Oh, I get it. So you're a genius and I'm a nincompoop. Right? Not much hope of teaching anything to a nincompoop, right?"

"You needn't put it like that. Let's just say that my life depends on getting the best blossoms I can. If they don't sell, I don't eat. Perhaps that's why the flowers grow so large—because I'm driven by necessity. People like you, on the other hand, who grow mums as a hobby, are motivated more by simple curiosity, or the desire to satisfy their pride."

"Oh, I see. You're telling me I should sell my mums too, is that it? Do you really think I'd stoop so low? How dare you say such a thing!"

"That's not what I'm saying at all. Why must you be this way?"

The relationship, in short, lacked a certain harmony.

As time went by, the Tōmotos' fortune only increased. When the new year came along they hired a team of carpenters and, without so much as consulting Sainosuke, began construction of a sizable mansion that extended from the rear of the garden to within an inch or so of his cottage. Sainosuke had just begun to consider severing relations again when, one day, Saburō came calling with a pensive and serious expression on his face.

"Please accept my sister as your bride," he said somberly.

Sainosuke could feel his cheeks burning. From the first time he'd laid eyes on the sister he'd been unable to dispel that image of tenderness and purity from his mind. But, true to form, his manly pride now forced him to launch into a queer sort of argument.

"I can't afford a betrothal gift, and I'm not qualified to take a bride like her anyway. You're rich people now, you know," he said, hiding his true feelings behind the sarcasm.

"Not at all. Everything we have is yours. That was how my sister intended it to be from the beginning. And there's no need to worry about a betrothal gift. All you have to do is move in with us, just as you are. My sister is in love with you."

Sainosuke shook his head, trying his best to feign composure. "Not interested. I have my own house. You won't catch me marrying into money. Not that I have anything against your sister, mind you," he said, and laughed in a way that he hoped sounded cavalier. "But to marry for money is the greatest shame a man can bring upon himself. I refuse. Go back and tell your sister that. And tell her that if she doesn't mind living in honest poverty, she can come move in with me."

Thus they parted once again on less than amicable terms. That night, however, along with a gentle breeze, a delicate white butterfly came fluttering into Sainosuke's room.

"I don't mind living in honest poverty," she said with a giggle. Her name was Kié.

For a while the two of them passed their days and nights within the confines of Sainosuke's ramshackle cottage, but eventually Kié opened a hole in the rear wall and another in the adjoining wall of the Tōmoto mansion, allowing her to go freely from one to the other. And, to

Sainosuke's great dismay, she also began to bring along whatever furnishings or utensils she needed.

"This won't do. That brazier, that vase . . . all these things are from your house. Don't you realize how it sullies a man's honor to use his wife's possessions? I want you to stop carting this junk over here."

Kié would only smile when he scolded her like this and continue to bring the things she needed. Sainosuke, who fancied himself a man of incorruptible integrity, finally resorted to purchasing a large ledger in which he wrote: "This is to acknowledge receipt of the following items, to be temporarily retained by the undersigned." He started trying to list every article Kié had brought from the mansion, but found to his chagrin that there was now nothing in the cottage that didn't fit that description. Realizing that he might fill any number of ledgers without completing the task, he gave up all hope. He continued to resent what was happening, however, and one night he turned to Kié and said: "Thanks to you I've ended up being a kept man. To acquire wealth through marriage is the greatest disgrace a man can suffer. For thirty years I've lived in noble, honest poverty, and now it's all been for nothing, thanks to you and that brother of yours."

The bitterness in his voice stung Kié's heart, and she looked at him sadly and said: "It's all my fault, I suppose. It's just that I wanted to do everything I could to find some way to repay you for your kindness. I'm afraid I didn't realize how committed you were to that honest poverty of yours. Let's do this: We'll sell all my things, and the new house as well. Then you can take the money and use it any way you like."

"Don't be stupid," he snapped at her. "You think a man like myself would accept your filthy money?"

"Well, then, what is to be done?" There was a sob in Kié's voice. "Saburō, too, feels a great debt of gratitude to you. That's why he works so hard to get money by growing the mums and delivering them all over town. What are we to do? We just don't see eye to eye on this at all, do we?"

"There's only one thing we can do: separate." Sainosuke's own high-minded pronouncements had backed him into a corner, and now he found himself having to utter these painful words, which were nowhere in his heart. "Let the pure live in moral purity and the corrupt in corruption. There's no other way. I'm not qualified to order anyone else about; I'll leave this place to you, build a little hut in the corner of the garden, and pass my days enjoying the solitary pleasures of honest poverty."

It was all quite ridiculous, but once a man has spoken there's no turning back. First thing the following morning Sainosuke slapped together a little lean-to in the corner of the garden. He moved into this tiny space that night and sat there on his knees, shivering in the cold. After he'd spent a mere two nights enjoying his honest poverty, however, the freezing temperatures began to take their toll, and on the third night he stole back to his cottage and tapped lightly on the rain shutter. It opened a crack and Kié's fair, smiling face appeared.

"So much for moral purity," she said with a giggle.

Sainosuke was deeply ashamed. From that night on, not a single obstinate demand would ever again escape his lips.

By the time the cherry trees along the Sumida River began to bloom, construction of the Tōmoto mansion was complete. It was now connected to the cottage in such a way that there was no distinction between the two. Sainosuke, however, offered not a word of complaint. He left the household affairs entirely up to Kié and Saburō, and spent his days playing Chinese chess with friends from the neighborhood.

One day the three members of the household set out for the Sumida to view the cherry blossoms. They settled down with their lunch at a suitable spot on the riverbank, and Sainosuke lost no time in breaking out the saké he'd brought and urging Saburō to join him. Kié shot a forbidding glance at her brother, but he calmly accepted a cup.

"Sis," he said, "it's all right if I have a drink or two today. We've saved up enough now so that you and Sainosuke can take it easy for the rest of your lives, even if I'm not around. I'm tired of growing chrysanthemums."

And with this mysterious declaration Saburō began guzzling saké at an alarming rate. He was soon thoroughly drunk, and finally he lay down and stretched out on the grass. And then, right before their eyes, his body melted away and disappeared in a puff of smoke, leaving nothing behind but his kimono and sandals. Flabbergasted, Sainosuke snatched up the kimono, only to find, growing out of the earth beneath it, a fresh, bright green chrysanthemum seedling. Now, for the first time, he realized that Saburō and Kié were not mere human beings. But Sainosuke, who by this time had come to truly appreciate the young pair's wisdom and affection, felt not in the least horrified at the realization. He only grew to love Kié, his poor chrysanthemum fairy, all the more deeply.

THE CHRYSANTHEMUM SPIRIT

When autumn came, Saburō's seedling, which Saino-suke had replanted in his garden, produced a single blossom. The flower was faintly rouge, like a drinker's blush, and gave off a light scent of saké. As for Kié, tradition tells us that there was "no change forever." In other words, she lived as a human being to the end of her days.

THE MERMAID
AND
THE SAMURAI

uring the reign of Emperor Gofukakusa, in the first year of the Hōji Era, on the twentieth day of the third month, a mermaid washed ashore at Oura in Tsugaru Province. The creature had a full head of long green hair, like strands of seaweed; its face, which bore a sorrowful expression, was that of a beautiful young woman, except for a small crimson cockscomb that adorned the center of its forehead; its upper body was transparent, like crystal, with a slight bluish tinge; its breasts were like two red berries of the nandina bamboo; its lower body resembled that of a fish and was covered with tiny scales like golden flower petals; its tail fin was translucent yellow and in the shape of an enormous ginkgo leaf; and its voice was as clear and resonant as the song of a skylark. This story has been handed down to us as a reminder of the strange and mysterious things to be found in our world, but the fact is that any number of wondrous creatures inhabit the northern seas to this day.

Long ago, in the fiefdom of Matsumae, there lived a samurai named Chūdō Konnai, a man of great courage and unquestionable integrity, who served as administrator of the coastal areas. One day in winter, while making the rounds of the beaches of Matsumae, Konnai came to the inlet of Sakegawa, and there at dusk he boarded a ferry with five or six other passengers in hopes of reaching the next port before dark. When they set out, the weather was fair and the waters smooth and placid, which was rare for winter in the north, but as the shore was receding behind them, the seas suddenly grew wild and angry, in spite of the fact that there was still no wind to speak of, and the boat was tossed about like a cork on the waves.

The passengers turned pale with fear and began raising a great commotion: One man cried out the name of the woman he loved, shouting "Farewell! Farewell!" while trembling like a frightened dog; another pulled from his basket a sutra to Kannon, the Goddess of Mercy, raised it to his forehead, oblivious to the fact that he was holding it upside-down, then spread it out and read it aloud in a quavering voice; another grabbed his gourd of saké and guzzled down every last drop, saying that death was one thing but he couldn't bear the thought of letting good wine go to waste, then dangling before the others the empty gourd, no larger than his hand, and solemnly declaring that, besides, it would make an excellent flotation device; another, for reasons of his own, no doubt, fervently licked the tip of his finger and rubbed the spittle on his forehead; another rummaged anxiously through his purse, counted his money, and, eyeing the other passengers suspiciously, growled that he was missing one ryō of gold; and yet another whiled away the moments before an almost certain death by trying to start an argument, claiming that someone had touched his knee. The waves, meanwhile, swelled to even greater size, and soon the boat began to bounce and shudder so violently that everyone fell silent, too terror-stricken even to scream. The captain was the first to succumb. "Have mercy upon us!" he groaned, plopping face down on the deck and lying there as still as a corpse while the others followed suit, collapsing in tears and finally fainting dead away.

THE MERMAID AND THE SAMURAI

Only Chūdō Konnai maintained his composure. He sat with his back to the gunwale, his legs crossed and his arms folded, peering silently ahead. Now the sea before him turned a golden hue and began to boil and erupt in bubbles of five distinct colors; the water parted in two rolling, white-capped waves; and from between them there emerged a mermaid, similar in every detail to the ones Konnai had heard tell of in stories, who tossed back her emerald curls with a shake of the head and began to snake toward the boat with astonishing speed, cutting through the water with swift, powerful strokes of her crystalline arms and opening her small red mouth to let out a single, piercing, whistle-like cry.

"Damnable wretch," Konnai muttered beneath his breath. "Obstruct the waterways, would you?" Furious, he took a small bow from his baggage, invoked the aid of Heaven, and launched an arrow. His aim was true; the arrow lodged in the mermaid's shoulder, and without so much as a startled cry she sank beneath the waves. And no sooner had she vanished than the troubled waters grew calm again. The setting sun was shining serenely upon the deck and the glassy sea when the captain finally rose to his knees, blinked, rubbed his eyes, simpered moronically, and said: "Well, I'll be damned. Must've been a dream."

Konnai was not the frivolous sort of samurai who would ever stoop to boasting of his own exploits. He said nothing, but sat back against the gunwale with folded arms and a quiet smile. One by one the other passengers lifted their pallid faces and looked about. One of them burst into a deafening cackle in hopes of hiding his own embarrassment, another shook his empty gourd and began grumbling about having wasted all that good

saké without even getting drunk, and the eighty-year-old
retired merchant, who moments ago had been trembling
uncontrollably and shouting the name of his young mistress back home, was now calmly adjusting the collar of
his kimono and instructing the others as to the nature
of their ordeal: "Well, that was a frightful experience,
what? Obviously we've just witnessed what is known as
the 'Dragon's Ascent,' a phenomenon often observed in
the seas off Etchū and Echizen, particularly during the
summer months. It begins with the sudden appearance
of a legion of dark clouds that descend toward the water,
while the water itself rises to meet the clouds, as if being
sucked through a hole in the sky, creating an enormous,
whirling, black pillar of water and clouds. And if you gaze
intently into that fearsome pillar you will clearly discern
the figure of a dragon ascending toward the heavens. So
it is written in a book I once read. I am also reminded of
another book, in which a man describes setting out from
Edo by sea. He relates that as the ship was plying the seas
off Okitsu, within sight of the Tōkaidō Road, a swarm of
black clouds swept down upon them. Greatly perturbed,
the captain of the ship declared that a dragon was trying
to pluck his vessel out of the sea and ordered all those
aboard to cut off their hair. The clipped locks were fed into
a fire, causing a mighty stench to rise skyward, and, lo and
behold, the black, swirling clouds above them scattered
and vanished in a twinkling. Were I myself a bit younger,
I would not have hesitated to cut off my own hair just
now, but unfortunately . . ." And with that he fell silent
and solemnly rubbed his hairless pate. "Oh, is that so?"
the sutra-chanter said in a voice dripping with sarcasm,
then turned away, muttering that any fool could see it was
all the doing of Kannon-sama, piously closed his eyes, and

began to chant: *Namu kanze ondai bosatsu*. "Ah! Here it is!" cried another ecstatically, digging the missing gold piece out from the folds of his kimono.

Not a man among them realized that they owed their very lives to Konnai, who merely sat with a half-smile on his face even as the ship at last came swaying gently into harbor and the passengers scrambled ashore, congratulating one another and celebrating with simple-minded whoops and cries.

It was not long after this incident that Chūdō Konnai arrived back at Matsumae Castle. Once he'd given a full report on his coastal inspection tour to his superior, Noda Musashi, and the conversation had turned to matters of a more casual and private nature, Konnai offhandedly related, without embellishing the story in the least, all that had transpired in the seas off Sakegawa. Musashi, having long admired Konnai's honesty of character, did not doubt for a moment that he had in fact encountered such a wondrous creature. "A rare occurrence, indeed, in this day and age!" he exclaimed, slapping his knee. "Let us lose no time in reporting this affair to His Lordship!" Konnai blushed and protested that it was hardly a matter of such importance, but Musashi interrupted him, saying: "Nonsense! It's an extraordinary feat, the like of which has never been equaled in history. It is a tale that will serve as a great inspiration to the young men of our clan, and spur them on to greater efforts." He spoke emphatically, leaving no room for argument, and, urging the embarrassed Konnai to hurry, ushered him into the daimyo's presence.

It so happened that the other ranking retainers were also in attendance at the main hall that day, and when Noda Musashi, still in a state of considerable excitement, asked for their attention and began to recount in full detail the strange adventure that had befallen Konnai during his trip, prefacing his remarks by saying that he was about to describe a feat of unprecedented skill and courage, all present, including the daimyo himself, edged closer and hung on his every word. All, that is, but one—a man by the name of Aosaki Hyakuemon.

This Hyakuemon was the son of one Hyakunojō, who had devoted many years of loyal service to the daimyo as a chief retainer of the Matsumae clan. Upon his father's death Hyakuemon had inherited the same rank and stipend, in spite of the fact that he had done—and continued to do—nothing whatsoever to earn them, but rather lived a life of idleness and debauchery. So puffed up with pride in his lineage was he, that he held his fellow retainers in contempt and had always refused to marry, declaring whenever the subject arose that he could scarcely permit the daughter of some parvenu to assume the Aosaki name. He was now forty-one, however, and not a samurai in the land would have relinquished his daughter to such a man, though he were to beg on bended knee. Disgruntled by this state of affairs, for which he alone was to blame, Hyakuemon never lost an opportunity to seek retaliation by heaping derision upon other members of the clan. He was universally disliked, not only for his unsavory character but for his physical appearance, which was the very image of a pale blue demon from hell. He stood nearly six feet tall and was extraordinarily thin and bony, with fingers as long and slender as writing-brushes, small and deep-set eyes that flickered with a perverse greenish glow, a great hooked nose, hollow, sunken cheeks, and a perpetual frown of distaste.

THE MERMAID AND THE SAMURAI

Before Musashi had got more than midway through the tale of Konnai's adventure, this Hyakuemon laughed through his beaklike nose and turned to a young tea-server who sat hunched over timidly in the rear of the hall. 'Well, Gensai,' he said, "what do you make of this? Is it not rather questionable conduct to impose such a preposterous tale upon His Lordship? There are no monsters in this world, no unexplainable mysteries; the monkey's face is red, the dog has four feet: so it always has been and so it always will be. A mermaid, no less! Are we here to listen to fairy tales? A grown man, a man of supposed distinction, speaking of sea monsters with red coxcombs—well, I ask you!"

Hyakuemon's voice grew ever louder and harsher.

"What say you, Gensai? Even supposing these freakish lady-fish, these so-called mermaids, did inhabit the northern seas, to shoot such a creature with a bow and arrow one would need virtually supernatural powers. Your average, mediocre archer would not stand a chance! Birds have wings; fish have fins. To bring down a small bird in flight, or shoot a goldfish as it swims, is not easily done; but to fell a monster with a—what was it, a crystal body?—why, one would need the skill of Raikō, Tsuna, Hachirō, Tawara Tōda, and the God of Arms all rolled into one. I speak from experience. The goldfish in my fountain at home— you yourself have seen them, have you not? As you know, they enjoy but a shallow pool in which to flit about, and yet, just the other day, to while away the time, I unleashed some two hundred arrows at them with a child's bow— two *hundred* arrows—and failed to score a single hit. Let us hope that our Konnai here, finding himself caught in a

53

storm at sea, was not simply so frightened that he let fly his arrow at an old rotting log adrift on the waves!"

Thus Hyakuemon ranted on, ostensibly addressing the mortified young tea-server, who cringed and fidgeted as the man clutched at his sleeve, but speaking loudly enough to make certain the daimyo could hear his snide and calumnious remarks. Finally Noda Musashi, who had long harbored enmity toward Hyakuemon for his arrogant and brazen manner and could now no longer contain his wrath, spun about to face him.

"That is merely your lack of education speaking," he growled through clenched teeth. "Only someone who possesses nothing but the most superficial knowledge would categorically state that there are no mysteries, no monsters in this world. Japan is a sacred land, the land of the gods; wonders which defy the limits of human understanding are everyday occurrences here. The occasional appearance of marvelous and fantastic beings is only to be expected in a land with more than a thousand leagues of mountains and seashores and three thousand years of history, a land which, I need scarcely add, is by no means to be compared with the piddling fountain in your garden. In ancient times, during the reign of Emperor Nintoku, there lived in Hida a man with two faces, one on either side of his head; during Emperor Temmu's reign, a bull with twelve horns was raised at a mountain cottage in Tamba; and on the fifteenth day of the sixth month of the fourth year of Keiun, during the reign of Emperor Mommu, a demon with three heads who measured twenty-six feet in height and five feet across arrived on these shores from a foreign land. With precedents such as these, you have no cause to doubt the existence of this mermaid."

THE MERMAID AND THE SAMURAI

As Musashi reeled off this rebuttal in the torrential, eloquent flow of words for which he was renowned, Hyakuemon's pale face went even paler, and finally, with a scornful sneer, he replied: "Superficial knowledge? If anyone is guilty of that, it is you, sir. But I am not fond of debate. Debates are for ignoble souls such as yourself who are anxious to achieve distinction. We are not children; we might exchange empty theories until we're out of breath and merely end up adhering all the more stubbornly to our respective views. Arguing is a foolish waste of time. I'm not saying that there cannot possibly be such things as mermaids in this world; I'm merely saying that I've never seen one, and that it's a pity that, in addition to his amusing tale, Konnai didn't bring this marvel along with him to present before His Lordship."

Musashi, enraged no less by the loathsome and provoking disdain with which Hyakuemon spoke than by the words themselves, edged closer to him and said: "To a true samurai, trust is everything. He who will not believe without seeing is a pitiful excuse for a man. Without trust, how can one know what is real and what is not? Indeed, one may see and yet not believe—is this not the same as never seeing? Is not everything, then, no more than an immaterial dream? The recognition of any reality begins with trust. And the source of all trust is love for one's fellow man. But you—you have not a speck of love in your miserable heart, nor of faith. Behold how honest Konnai, the blameless target of your venomous tongue, trembles with rage, wringing bitter tears from the depths of his faithful soul. Konnai is not, like yourself, sir, a man to whom it would ever occur to resort to prevarication. Surely not even you can claim to be unaware of his unwavering fidelity over the years."

Thus Musashi pressed his case, but Hyakuemon merely ignored him and pointed toward the front of the hall. "Look there!" he barked. "His Lordship is taking his leave. He does not appear to be amused." Hyakuemon prostrated himself before the daimyo as the latter retired to his inner chambers, but he could not resist having the final word. "Insufferable fools," he muttered as he rose to his feet once the daimyo had gone. "You may wish to give the name 'honesty' to what others would call dimwittedness, but leave it to such 'honest men' as yourselves to deceive the world with your fabulous dreams and superstitions." And with that, he left the hall, creeping off as silently as a cat.

As for the other retainers present, some despised Hyakuemon for his mean-spirited pettiness, while others considered Musashi's eloquence sheer affectation and felt that neither was worth siding with, and still others, who'd been dozing throughout, merely climbed woozily to their feet, oblivious to all that had transpired. By ones and twos they left the hall until none but Musashi and Konnai remained. Musashi gnashed his teeth in vexation.

"How the wretch prattles on!" he growled. "Konnai, I can guess what is in your heart. As the true samurai that you are, you realize there is but one course of action; but know that whatever comes of this, I, Musashi, will take your side. In any case, such insolence must not go unpunished."

These words of encouragement, stouthearted though they were, only left Konnai feeling all the more keenly the hopelessness of his situation, and for some moments, wracked with mournful sobs, he could make no reply at all. Such it is for those in the grips of misfortune: declarations of support and sympathy, rather than providing comfort, may serve only to increase the victim's pain. Overwhelmed with despair, Konnai bowed his head and wept, even as he resigned himself to the fact that his life was all but over. At length, wiping the tears away with both fists, he looked up and spoke in a voice still punctuated with sobs:

"Thank you. The abuse which Hyakuemon has heaped upon me today is scarcely such as I can find it in me to ignore. I assure you that, though I may be his inferior in terms of rank, my only thought was: Knave! I shall slice you in two! Being in the presence of His Lordship, however, I had no choice but to endure the unendurable and choke back these tears of rage. But make no mistake—I am resolved to do what must be done. To chase the bastard Hyakuemon down at this very moment and dispense of his life with one stroke of my sword would be easy enough; but then the world would believe I'd shed his blood out of anger that he'd exposed my lie. My account of the mermaid would come to be regarded with even greater suspicion, which could not but reflect unfavorably upon yourself as well. Since, in any case, this life of mine is lost, I shall delay the end only long enough to return to the inlet at Sakegawa, where, if the God of Arms has not forsaken me, I will recover the carcass of that mermaid, bring it back to the castle for all to see, rebuke Hyakuemon with an easy mind, cut him down, and then gladly commit *seppuku*."

Such was the pathos of this speech that Musashi too began to weep. "Would I had never meddled in your affairs!" he said. "Announcing your heroic feat before His Lordship was a grave error. To think that all for some meaningless debate over mermaids, a worthy man must die! Forgive me, Konnai. May you not be born a samurai in the next life!" Turning his tear-stained face away, Musashi rose to his feet. "I shall look after your household in your absence," he said gruffly, and strode out of the hall.

Konnai's wife had died of an illness some six years before, and he now shared his house with his only daughter and a maidservant. The daughter, Yaé, was a tall and sturdy girl of sixteen with fair skin and lovely features; the maidservant, whose name was Mari, was a petite and clever young woman some twenty-one years of age. Konnai returned home that day making every effort to appear carefree and cheerful. "I must leave immediately on another trip," he said, "and I may be gone quite a while this time. Watch out for each other." And without another word, he surreptitiously gathered up most of his savings, stuffed the money into his clothes, and dashed out of the house.

"Father's acting awfully strange," Yaé said, after seeing him off.

"Yes, he is," Mari calmly agreed. Konnai was inept when it came to deceiving people, and his smiling, light-hearted pose had been of no avail; both his sixteen-year-old daughter and the maidservant had seen right through it.

"And why would he take all that gold?" wondered Yaé. They'd even seen him snatch up his savings.

Mari nodded pensively and muttered: "It must be something rather serious."

"I'm frightened." Yaé placed her hands over her breast. "My heart is pounding."

The Mermaid and the Samurai

"There's no telling what might happen," Mari said. "We must prepare the house for any eventuality."

They were rolling up their sleeves to begin cleaning the house when Noda Musashi slipped in through the back door, unaccompanied and dressed in a plain kimono.

"Has your father left already?" he whispered to Yaé.

"Yes. And he took all his gold and silver with him."

Musashi forced a grim smile. "It may be a rather long trip. If you should need anything at all while he's gone, you mustn't hesitate to come to me." He pressed a large sum of money into her hands. "This should hold you for the time being."

Certain now that her father was in some sort of trouble, Yaé, samurai child that she was, slept that night in her kimono, with the sash firmly tied, hugging a dagger to her breast.

Konnai reached Sakegawa the following morning. His first order of business was to assemble all the fishermen in the village and distribute among them every last piece of the silver and gold he'd brought.

"I speak to you not in my official capacity, but as an individual in a difficult predicament," he began, dutifully making that important distinction. "It is in regard to a personal and confidential matter," he continued, then faltered and blushed. With a rueful smile, prefacing his remarks with a defensive "You may not believe what I'm about to tell you," and shouting to be heard over the howling wind that pelted the seashore with snow, he proceeded to recount the entire affair of the mermaid, ending with a desperate plea: "This is the request of a lifetime. I beseech

59

you to recover that mermaid's carcass for me. If I do not present it to a certain man, I, Konnai, will lose face as a samurai, and my honor will be blighted forever. It's cold weather for such work, I know, but I beg you to spare no efforts until we've retrieved that monster's body."

The elderly fishermen sympathized, believing Konnai's story without question, and while it must be admitted that the younger men had their doubts about mermaids and such, they too were at least curious enough to join in casting the great nets and dragging the bottom of the inlet. Unfortunately, all they managed to snag that day were common herring, cod, crabs, sardines, and flatfish—nothing the least bit out of the ordinary—and the same was true the following day and the day after that. Though every man in the village participated, enduring all manner of hardship, bobbing about in their boats, battered by wind and waves, casting their nets, and diving into the icy waters, it was all in vain, and finally, toward the end of the third day, the younger men began to complain as they stood around the fires on the beach, making loud, vulgar jokes—"Just look at that samurai's eyes, he ain't normal I tell you, he's loony is what he is, and we're crazy for takin' a lunatic at his word and divin' into that freezin' water. Me, I've had enough, I quit. Why should I be out here lookin' for some sea mermaid we'll never find when I could be gettin' warm in the arms of my land mermaid back in the village?"

As the young men roared with laughter, Konnai sat a short distance away, alone in his torment, pretending not to hear and concentrating his entire being on the fervent prayers he offered up to the deities of the sea. "Let me retrieve but a single golden scale or a single strand of hair from that monster," he prayed, "so that I may preserve my honor, and that of Musashi as well, and together we can reproach Hyakuemon to our heart's content, after which I shall give him a taste of the blade of truth, deliver him his just punishment, and dispel from my heart these bitter clouds of rancor."

Moved by the pathetic sight of Konnai forlornly stretching his neck to peer from one end of the inlet to the other, an elderly fisherman approached with tears of pity welling up in his eyes. "Now, now," he said. "Everything'll work out just fine, don't you worry, mister samurai, sir. Those youngsters don't know what they're talkin' about, but we older fellows, we figure there's sure enough a mermaid down there with the good samurai's arrow stickin' out of her, because, see, the seas around here, hell, they've always been full of the strangest fish, ever since way back when. Why, when we were boys, listen, right here off this shore, we sometimes used to see this giant old fish that people called the okina, and, oh my, what a commotion there used to be over that! I'm not lyin' when I tell you the damn thing was five, six miles long, maybe longer—nobody knows for sure how big it was 'cause nobody ever saw it all in one piece—but when that monster come around, why, the sea would start a-rumblin' like a thunderstorm and the waves would swell up like mountains, even if there weren't no wind, and all the whales, why, they'd scatter in every direction, fleein' for their lives, and the fishermen would start screamin' 'Okina! Yah! It's the okina!' and row toward shore as fast as they could, and then finally that fish would rise to the surface, and I'm tellin' you it looked like a whole string of islands had suddenly popped out of the sea. Yes, sir, there's some frightenin' strange fish and monsters out in these waters, always

61

has been, just ask anybody who's lived around here long enough, which is why there's no doubt in our minds that you saw what you say you saw, and I'll tell you one thing for sure: We're goin' to find that mermaid's body for you. You won't have to lose your face or nothin' like that."

The old fisherman brushed the snow off Konnai's shoulders as he delivered these naive yet earnest words of encouragement, but his kindness only left the samurai feeling all the more forlorn. Alas! Has it come to this? Have I fallen so far as to receive the pity of an old and ignorant fisherman? Thus Konnai asked himself bitterly, even twisting the old man's meaning, convincing himself that behind his kind words was a sense of hopelessness and resignation. "I beg of you!" he shouted, scrambling to his feet. "I really did shoot a monstrous fish in the waters of this inlet. I swear by the God of Arms I did! I implore you. Please don't give up until you've found at least a strand of that mermaid's hair, or a scale from her freakish body!"

And with that he kicked at a pile of drifted snow and ran off down the beach to where the fishermen were packing up their things and preparing to call it a day. "I beg you!" he cried, grabbing one of them by the arm, his eyes wild and desperate. "Just a short while longer!" But the fishermen, having been paid beforehand, were running out of enthusiasm; they halfheartedly tossed their nets in the shallows near the shore a few more times, then began disappearing by ones and twos until there was not so much as a stray dog left on the beach.

Even after the sun went down and the north wind began to blow with still greater force, whipping the snow into a blinding blizzard, Konnai continued to pace back and forth, stamping his feet on the deserted shoreline until long after midnight, when, rather than retreating to the village, he took shelter as he had each night from the start in a little boathouse next to the water, dozing there for only a short time and then, well before dawn, running back out again to the beach. Spying a drifting tangle of seaweed and mistaking it for his prey, he would rejoice momentarily, only to shed bitter tears when, soon enough, he realized his mistake. Then, spotting a piece of driftwood near the shore, he would splash out into the surf with a glimmer of hope, only to return to the beach with a sinking heart. Since arriving at Sakegawa he had been intent only on finding the mermaid's remains and had scarcely eaten, as a result of which his mind had grown so beclouded that he now began to wonder if he really had seen a mermaid that time, if he wasn't merely deceiving himself into thinking that he'd shot such a creature, or if it hadn't been only a dream after all—doubts that left him laughing madly, deliriously, as he stood there alone on the snow-covered beach. Ah, he thought, if only I had fainted dead away like the other passengers on the boat and had never laid eyes on that cursed creature; it is simply because of my reckless indifference to peril that I witnessed such a wonder of nature and must suffer like this! How I envy those self-satisfied commoners who, seeing nothing and comprehending nothing, are convinced they know it all! There are in this world things of such mystery and awesome beauty that the small-minded cannot even imagine them. There are, yet he who discovers them risks falling into a bottomless hell. I must have done something heinous in a previous life, to have accumulated such karma. Or perhaps I was born beneath an evil star that destined me to a wretched and ignominious death. If so, why delay it any longer? Why not just throw myself into these crashing, rocky waters and hope to be reborn a mermaid?

With head bowed, he stumbled along the beach, seemingly already in Death's grasp yet still unable to abandon hope of finding the mermaid's carcass. As the sky became imbued with the pale first light of dawn, he sighed heavily and thought, in all seriousness: Ah, if nothing else, let me at least behold that okina of which the old man spoke!

And so we leave our unfortunate hero, confused and ranting incoherently, apparently out of his senses and, from the look of things, unlikely to live much longer.

Back at home, Yaé had been offering constant prayers to all gods and buddhas for the safe return of her father, but when three days, then four days passed without any hint as to his fate, save for a series of minor but ominous mishaps—a teacup dropped and smashed, the breaking of a sandal thong, a pine branch in the garden snapping under the weight of only a thin layer of snow—she found herself unable to remain sitting at home, and when the sun went down she stole to Musashi's house, where she ascertained that her father's destination had been the inlet at Sakegawa. That same night she made preparations and set out with the maidservant Mari to find him. Making their way along the midnight road by the light of a freshly fallen snow, resting under the eaves of houses or snuggling together for warmth in caves by the sea, dozing off to the sound of the waves before once again leaping up to continue their journey, urging each other on but, being women, making slow progress, the mistress and her servant did not reach Sakegawa until the evening of the third day. There, they staggered to the seashore only to find, to their unspeakable horror, Konnai, now a cold and withered corpse, stretched out on a mat of coarse straw. They were told that his body had been discovered drifting near the shore that morning, his head so entangled with seaweed that at first he was mistaken for the mermaid he'd claimed to have shot.

Yaé and Mari fell upon Konnai's body from either side and clung to him, too grief-stricken to speak and sobbing with such passion that even the thick-skinned fishermen turned away, unable to watch. Yaé, whose mother was long dead and who now found herself abandoned by her father as well, wept uncontrollably, nearly out of her mind with grief. But finally, having come to a great resolve in her heart, she lifted her pale face and said: "Mari. We too must die."

"Yes," Mari said, nodding.

They stood up quietly, and just then there came to their ears the thunder of a horse's hooves and the powerful voice of Noda Musashi calling to them as he galloped down to the seashore. Dismounting, Musashi stood over the body of Konnai and hung his head.

"What an abominable waste. Has it come to this, then? Shit! What care I for mermaids now? Musashi is not amused; Musashi is very, very angry, and when Musashi is angry, he is not to be reasoned with. He can be the most unreasonable of men. Whether mermaids exist or not is of no importance now. All that matters is that a certain vile bastard be punished. You, fishermen! Bring horses for these two women. Now! Find a pair of horses and bring them here, damn you!"

After thus directing his rage at the commoners milling about nearby, Musashi turned to glare at Yaé.

65

"And you! Stop that sobbing! There is work to do, revenge to be exacted. If we don't return immediately, burst into Hyakuemon's home, relieve him of his foul head, and bring it back to present to Konnai, I shall not permit you to refer to yourself as the daughter of a samurai. Enough of your sniveling!"

"Hyakuemon?" Mari took a step forward and cocked her head to one side. "Do you mean Aosaki Hyakuemon?"

"Of course. Who else would it be?"

"In that case," Mari said calmly, "I begin to see . . . For some time now this Aosaki, old as he is, has had his heart set on my mistress. He's been very insistent that she become his bride. My mistress, naturally, says that she would die before she'd marry a man with a nose like that. Not, of course, that the master was about to permit such a—"

"So that's it. That explains everything. The worm had the temerity to claim to be a confirmed bachelor, a woman hater, when in fact he was a rejected lover all along. How despicable. The man is absolutely beneath contempt. To lash out at Konnai in retaliation for his own wounded feelings is worse than loathsome—it's ludicrous. Ha!" Musashi shouted triumphantly. "The preposterous fool!"

That night, with Musashi leading the way, the two young women stole into Hyakuemon's home, halberds in hand. They found their enemy in a room in the rear, drinking saké with a concubine. Musashi, with one stroke of his sword, lopped off Hyakuemon's long and spindly right arm. Hyakuemon didn't so much as wince, however, even as his severed arm dropped to the floor, but made to unsheathe his own sword with his left hand. Mari stepped in from the side and kicked his legs out from under him, but he rose to his knees, still undaunted, and thrust his sword at Yaé. With a gasp of astonishment, Musashi sank his own blade into Hyakuemon's shoulder, and he fell, sprawling backward but, far from giving up the ghost, writhed about on the floor like a snake, pulled a dagger from his sash, and hurled it with vicious force at Yaé, who barely managed to dodge its path. She and Musashi exchanged a dumbfounded glance, amazed at the tenacity of their foe, before finishing him off.

Once they'd accomplished their mission, Yaé and Mari hurried with Hyakuemon's head to Sakegawa, where Konnai's body still lay. Musashi, meanwhile, returned to his home and wrote out the details of the entire vendetta, expressing remorse for the great crime of putting Hyakuemon to death without first receiving permission from the daimyo, and claiming all responsibility for what had occurred. Then, after commanding his servant to deliver the document to the castle first thing in the morning, he performed seppuku without the least hesitation, thus ending his life in a manner worthy of the excellent and admirable samurai that he was.

After presenting Konnai with his enemy's severed head and then seeing him buried with due ceremony, the two women returned home, where they closed the front gate and ensconced themselves within the house to await the daimyo's verdict. Dressed in immaculate white kimono, they too were prepared to take their own lives should that be the judgment. In due time a council of chief retainers announced their decision: Hyakuemon himself had been such a perverse man as to qualify as an unnatural monster of this world; and since Musashi had taken responsibility for the incident and had already carried out his own punishment, there was nothing untoward in considering the affair a private dispute that had been settled in a satisfactory manner. The daimyo approved this decision and even praised the two women for the laudable manner in which they'd avenged their father and master. Shortly thereafter, Yaé was wed to Imura Sakunosuke, youngest son of the ranking retainer Sakuemon. Her groom took the Chūdō family name as his own, thereby assuring the continuation of Konnai's lineage. Soon thereafter, the maidservant Mari became the bride of a handsome young assistant law enforcement official named Toi Ichizaemon.

Late one night about a hundred days after Konnai's death, a dispatch arrived at the castle from Kasuga Shrine, located at the seaside in Kitaura:

> A most peculiar skeleton was discovered washed up on the shore here today. The flesh has rotted away, leaving only bones, but the upper half of the body is very much like that of a human being, while the lower half is unmistakably that of a fish. Although no explanation is yet available, it was deemed that such an extraordinary discovery should be reported at once. . . .

An administrator was immediately sent to Kitaura to investigate. He ascertained that the strange skeleton was indeed that of a mermaid, and that embedded in its shoulder was the tip of one of Chūdō Konnai's famous arrows. Thus that spring was a season of twofold joy for Yaé, and thus ends this story affirming certain victory for those with the power to believe.

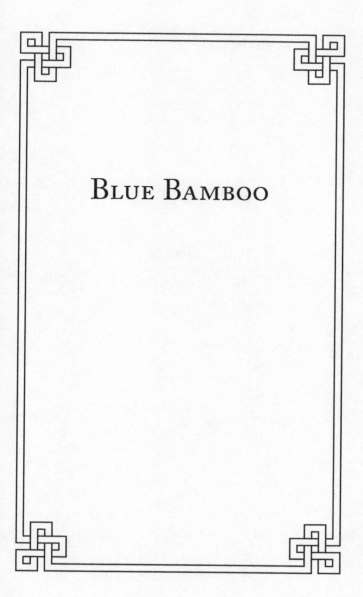

BLUE BAMBOO

nce upon a time, in a certain district in Hu-
nan, there lived an impoverished scholar
named Yü Jung. Poverty and scholarship
have always gone hand in hand, it seems,
and one can't help but wonder why that
might be. Consider Yü Jung for example. Far from being
of low birth or inferior breeding, he was in fact a man of
rather handsome features with an air of genuine refinement. And though it might be overstating things to claim
that he loved books the way some men love love, he had
faithfully followed the path of learning since his earliest
days, never engaging in any improper behavior to speak
of. Yet he was simply not one of those upon whom fortune
had ever seen fit to smile.

Yü Jung's parents had both passed away when he was
a child, and he had been brought up in the care of a succession of relatives who shuttled him from one home to
the next. Once his inheritance was exhausted, however,
these relatives began to look upon him as little more than
a nuisance, and finally one of his uncles, a drunkard who
was well in his cups at the time, pressed upon the young
man a dark-complected, skinny, and uneducated maidservant from his own home, arrogantly ordering him to take
her as his bride and pronouncing it an excellent match. Yü
Jung was thoroughly repulsed by the proposition, but the
uncle was, after all, one of the relatives who'd raised him
and a person to whom he therefore felt a lifelong obliga-

tion. Being a man for whom filial piety was the highest law, Yü Jung could scarcely vent his anger at this outrageous imposition, and so, fighting back the tears and feeling more dead than alive, he meekly suffered himself to be wed to that skinny, withered, hideous woman two years his senior who, to add insult to injury, was rumored to be the drunken uncle's mistress.

Ugly as this woman may have been, by no means did she compensate for it with a gentle heart. She had nothing but scorn for Yü Jung's scholarship, and when she heard him muttering something to the effect that "The Way of Great Learning leads to the highest excellence," she laughed through her nose and said, with all the sarcasm and malice she could muster, "Excellence? Better a way that leads to a little money, or a decent meal," then slapped a bundle of her own dirty laundry in his face and added: "Look here, these need washing. It wouldn't hurt you to help me out around here now and then."

Yü Jung tucked the clothing under his arm and headed for the riverbed behind the house, reciting a poem beneath his breath as he went:

> *A whinnying of horses*
> *As daylight wanes.*
> *A clash of swords;*
> *The first breath of autumn.*

The poem did little to relieve his sense of the dreariness of life, however, or the feeling that he was an exile in the land of his own birth, and with a great, gaping emptiness in his heart he wandered aimlessly up and down the riverbank, like a man bereft of his wits.

"Such a wretched way of life is an insult to my august ancestors," he thought. "This fall I will be thirty—the time when a man must stand firm. By heaven, I shall. I shall rise to the challenge and spare no effort until I have made a great name for myself!"

Having arrived at this momentous decision, Yü Jung strode back to his house, dealt his wife a resounding blow, and marched off to the capital, brimming with confidence, to sit for the government service examination. Unfortunately, his many years as a starving scholar had robbed him of strength and focus; the answers he wrote were hopelessly garbled, and he failed the exam spectacularly. His sorrow, as he trudged wearily homeward, was more than mere words can convey, and since he hadn't eaten for some time, he was soon so famished he could scarcely walk. When he reached the King Wu Shrine, on the shore of Lake Tung-t'ing, he collapsed on the balcony in front of the main hall, sprawled on his back, and moaned.

"Ah, what is this world but a realm of meaningless suffering? Since childhood I have devoted myself to studying the Way of the ancient sages and have remained ever vigilant, even in solitude, against unworthy thoughts. And yet, though I may have grasped a truth or two from time to time, I have been granted none of heaven's blessings. Far from it: I've been subjected to ridicule and derision every day of my life. In spite of which, did I not take courage and boldly present myself at that examination? Yes! Only to fail miserably . . . In a world like this, where the brazen, the shameless, the evil-hearted alone prosper, a weak and penniless scholar like myself is destined forever to be a failure and a laughingstock. I struck my wife and dashed gallantly out of the house: that much was all to the good, but heaven knows how she'll lay into me when I return after failing in my heroic quest. Woe is me! I'd just as soon end it all right here and now."

Such was Yü Jung's exhaustion that his mind had become thoroughly befuddled, and thus, unworthy though it was of one who had studied the Way of the sages, he cursed the world and lamented his fate. Peering through droopy-lidded eyes at a great flock of crows that whirled about in the sky above him, he sighed and muttered: "Ah, to be one of those crows, who know nothing of wealth and poverty!" Then he closed his eyes and lay there as still as a corpse on the balcony of the King Wu Shrine.

Now, King Wu, you must know, was the posthumous title given to a great military leader of the Three Kingdoms era. After his death he was deified as the guardian spirit of waterways, which was why this shrine on the shore of Lake Tung-t'ing was dedicated to him. As deities go, King Wu was said to be remarkably responsive to prayers, and each time a ship passed his shrine the crew would bow their heads in worship. In the woods next to the shrine lived a flock of hundreds of crows, and whenever a ship appeared, the entire flock would take wing with a deafening din of caws and squawks to circle above the mast. The crew and passengers considered the crows sacred emissaries of the deity king and would fling scraps of mutton and other meats up into the air for them to catch in their beaks.

It was the sight of these birds frolicking merrily about in the great blue sky that had inspired Yü Jung's envy. "Ah, to be a crow. . . ." He muttered the words in a feeble, doleful voice, and he was just beginning to nod off when someone tapped him on the shoulder.

"Hello, there," said a man dressed in a thin black robe. Yü Jung, still half asleep, peered up at him.

"I'm sorry. Please don't yell at me. I meant no harm. So sorry . . ."

Apologizing to others for no reason whatsoever was second nature to Yü Jung, an ignoble habit born of having been scolded incessantly since childhood, and as he rolled over on his side and closed his eyes again he continued to mutter, "So sorry, so sorry," as if in a delirium.

"No one's going to yell at you," said the man in the black robe. His voice was a strange, hoarse sort of cackle. "I've been sent by King Wu. His Majesty wishes me to inform you that if you find the world of human beings so disagreeable, and so envy these crows the life they lead, then you're just the man we've been looking for. It happens that there is a vacancy among the Black Robes, and His Majesty has condescended to bestow the appointment upon you. Here."

So saying, the man covered Yü Jung with a thin black garment exactly like his own, and in less time than it takes to say it, Yü Jung was transformed into a crow. He blinked, hopped up onto the balustrade, and began to comb out his feathers with his beak. Then he spread his wings and flew off, somewhat falteringly at first, to join the flock swirling in the air above a passing ship whose sails shone white in the light of the setting sun.

Swooping left and right, he deftly caught the scraps of meat sailors flung up; soon his stomach was fuller than he could recall it ever having been in his life, and he flew back to the woods beside the temple and perched on the branch of a tree. As he sharpened his beak on the branch, he gazed at the late afternoon sunlight glittering like gold on the surface of Lake Tung-t'ing. The sight moved him to recite a poem in the manner of the ancient sages:

Like a thousand golden petals:
Wavelets scattered
By the autumn wind.

"Am I to take it, sir," said an alluring feminine voice, "that you are pleased?"

Yü Jung turned to see a female crow perched next to him on the branch. He bowed politely to her.

"'Pleased' is scarcely the word, miss. Never have I known such lightness, such a sense of being free of the dust and dirt of the world." After saying this, he reflexively added: "I'm sorry. I don't know what to say."

"I understand," said the other in a calm and soothing tone. "I'm told you've had a very difficult life. I know how you must feel. But you'll be fine now. I won't let anyone hurt you."

"Oh? Forgive me, but . . . May I ask whom I have the honor of addressing?"

"Why, I'm to be your companion. Whatever you desire, you have only to ask. I'm here to serve your every need. Or . . . do I displease you?"

"Displease me? Certainly not, but . . ." Rattled, Yü Jung cast about for the proper words. "I have a wife of my own, you see. The superior man must abstain from lascivious conduct. I won't be led into temptation," he declared, trying to look the part of a crow of the highest morality.

"I beg your pardon, sir! Do you imagine that some base and frivolous passion has inspired me to approach you like this? You do me an injustice. I am here at the bidding of His Majesty, the benevolent Wu. It is he who has commanded me to offer you solace and comfort. Understand that you are no longer a human being, and that the wife you had in your other life is no longer a consideration. She may be a gentle and loving soul, but I assure you that I will prove in no way inferior. I shall devote myself wholeheartedly to serving you, and you will find that avian fidelity is based upon an even higher and purer truth than that of humans. Unworthy though I may seem to you now, I beg you to allow me to stay by your side. My name is Blue Bamboo."

Yü Jung was deeply moved.

"Thank you. I have suffered much at the hands of human society. Forgive me if I seem overly suspicious. I am unaccustomed to such kindness, you see, and scarcely know how to accept it gracefully. Do forgive me."

"My! You needn't speak so formally. It sounds odd. Don't you see? I'm to be your wife. Would you fancy an after-dinner stroll, my lord?"

Yü Jung nodded in as lordly a manner as he could manage, and said: "Lead the way, Blue Bamboo."

"Come, then," she said, and took to the sky.

Calling back and forth, now one in the lead and now the other, with the autumn wind soft beneath their wings, the hazy waters of Lake Tung-t'ing far below them, the tiled roofs of distant Yüeh Yang Pagoda glistening in the fiery glow of the setting sun, and the reflection of the surrounding mountains embossed on the shimmering surface of the Hsiang River, the black-robed newlyweds flew wherever their hearts inclined, strangers to anxiety, delusion, or fear, and when they tired they rested their wings atop the mast of a homeward bound ship and looked into each other's eyes and smiled. When night fell at last they winged leisurely back toward the woods, admiring the sight of Lake Tung-t'ing bathed in the brilliant light of the autumn moon, and when they reached their roost they nestled together and slept. The following morning they splashed about in the waters of the lake, bathing their feathers and rinsing their throats, then darted off toward an approaching ship and breakfasted on the sailors' morning offering. Blue Bamboo, the demure and innocent bride of our failed examinee, was ever at his side, sticking as close to him as a shadow and gently looking after his every need. Yü Jung felt as if all the misery of his life had been swept away without a trace.

By the afternoon of that day, he was completely at home in his new role and had mastered the art of flitting about above the masts of passing ships, and when a vessel laden with soldiers came along he ignored his companions, who fled, squawking of danger, and paid no heed to Blue Bamboo's cries of warning, too full of himself and the freedom of flight to resist the temptation to circle proudly in the air above it. He did not notice until too late that one of the soldiers had drawn a bow and was taking aim, and in the next moment an arrow pierced his breast. He fell from the sky like a stone. Blue Bamboo raced to him with lightning speed, caught him under one wing, and carried him back to the balcony of the King Wu Shrine, where she laid him down and clung to him, shedding a flood of tears as she tried to tend to his wound. The damage was too severe, however, and Blue Bamboo, seeing that her husband was beyond hope, let out a keening, mournful cry to summon the rest of the flock. Learning what had just occurred, the flock took to the air with a great flapping of wings to surround the soldiers' ship and fan the water, roiling the surface with tremendous waves that in no time at all caused the vessel to capsize and sink. Thus avenged, the great flock of crows lifted their voices in a triumphant song that resounded across the entire lake. Blue Bamboo hurried back to Yü Jung's side and gently pressed her cheek against his.

"Do you hear that?" she whispered plaintively. "Do you hear the victory song of your comrades?"

The pain in Yü Jung's breast was insufferable. He opened his unseeing eyes and with his dying breath murmured:

"Blue Bamboo . . ."

And with that he awoke to find that he was once again a man, the same impoverished scholar as before, lying on the balcony of the King Wu Shrine. The setting sun burned brightly on the maple trees in the woods before him, where hundreds of crows were innocently hopping from twig to twig, playing and laughing.

"Finally woke up, did you?"

An old man dressed in peasant clothing smiled down at him.

"Who . . . Who are you?" said Yü Jung.

"Me? I'm just a farmer from down the road. I passed by here yesterday evening and found you lying there, dead to the world. I called out to you as loud as I could, but you wouldn't wake up. Shook you by the shoulders and everything—you just snored away, smiling to yourself every now and then. I was worried even after I got home, so I kept coming back to check on you. You're pale as a ghost, you know that? You sick or something?"

"No. No, I'm not sick." Nor, oddly enough, was he hungry now. "Sorry," he said, apologizing as usual, then sat up on his knees and bowed politely to the farmer. "This is very embarrassing," he began, and proceeded to explain how he'd come to be lying there asleep on the balcony, finishing with a final, "I'm terribly sorry."

The farmer gazed at Yü Jung with compassionate eyes, then took out his purse and handed him a small sum of money.

"Inscrutable are the ways of heaven," he said. "Bestir yourself and leap back into the fray. In our seventy years of life, no one knows what might occur. Every ebb has its flow. The heart of man is as changeable as the storm-tossed waves of Lake Tung-t'ing."

After offering this unexpectedly eloquent advice, the farmer turned and walked off. Yü Jung felt as if he were still dreaming. He stood and gazed vacantly after the old man, then turned to peer up at the crows assembled on the branches of the maple trees.

"Blue Bamboo!" he shouted. Startled, the crows all sprang as one from their roosts with a great cacophony of cries. They briefly circled the sky over Yü Jung's head, then sped out toward the lake and were gone.

So it was just a dream, Yü Jung thought sadly. He shook his head, breathed a deep sigh, and dejectedly set out for home.

BLUE BAMBOO

No one there seemed to have missed him much. His cold-hearted wife lost no time in setting him to work, ordering him to haul some boulders to his uncle's garden. Dripping with sweat, Yü Jung pushed, rolled, and carried any number of enormous rocks from the riverbed, mournfully recalling what Confucius had said: *To be poor without resentment is difficult indeed*. "Willingly would I die in the evening," he muttered repeatedly to himself, nostalgic for the happy life he'd experienced in his dream, "could I but hear the voice of Blue Bamboo in the morning."

Po-i and Shu-ch'i did not keep the former wickedness of men in mind, Confucius tells us, *and hence the resentments directed toward them were few*. Our Yü Jung too, possessing as he did the lofty-mindedness of one who aspires to the way of the superior man, made at first every effort to refrain from despising his heartless relatives or speaking out against the uneducated hag who was his wife, preferring to bury himself in the classics, cultivating refinement and purity of taste. In time, however, the contempt to which he was relentlessly subjected became more than he could bear, and during the spring of the third year since his return he delivered another blow to his wife's head. "Just watch me. I'm going to be somebody," he said, and marched off, bursting with noble ambitions, to sit once again for the government exam.

Unfortunately, he failed it this time too. It seems our hero simply wasn't much good at taking tests. On his way back home, he stopped again at the King Wu Shrine on the banks of his now-beloved Lake Tung-t'ing. Everything his eyes beheld brought back delightful memories, but these only served to increase his sorrow a thousand-fold, and standing there before the shrine he began to weep and lament at the top of his voice. When the sobs finally subsided, he took what little money he had in his pocket and purchased some scraps of mutton, and these he scattered in the courtyard as an offering to the sacred crows. He watched them swoop down from the trees to peck at the meat and wondered if Blue Bamboo was among them. But the ebony-feathered birds all looked so alike that he was unable even to tell male from female.

"Which one of you is Blue Bamboo?" he said, but not a single crow so much as looked up at him; the scraps of mutton enjoyed their undivided attention. Yü Jung wasn't ready to admit defeat, however. "If Blue Bamboo is among you, let her remain last," he announced, his voice choked with immeasurable longing.

Soon the mutton was gone. Two of the crows flew back to the woods, then a group of five, and so on, until only three remained searching the ground for meat. Seeing this, Yü Jung felt his heartbeat quicken and his palms begin to perspire, but once these last three had ascertained that not a scrap was left, they too flew off without so much as a backward glance. So great was Yü Jung's disappointment that he grew dizzy and nearly fainted, but still he found it impossible to tear himself away. He sat down on the balcony and let out sigh after sigh, as he watched the mists of spring crawling over the surface of the lake.

"Now that I've failed the examination twice in a row, how am I to return home with any dignity whatsoever? My life is not worth living. I'm told that long ago, during the epoch of the Warring States, valiant Ch'ü Yüan, the father of poetry, threw himself into these very waters and drowned, shouting: 'The world is drunk; I alone perceive the truth!' If I were to drown myself in Lake Tungt'ing, this sea of sweet memories, who knows but that Blue Bamboo might be watching somewhere and weep for me? Blue Bamboo is the only one who has ever loved me. All the others in my life are nothing but dreadful, self-seeking ogres. 'Every ebb has its flow'—so that old man said to encourage me three years ago, but it was a lie. People born to misery are destined to remain forever in misery. Is this what it means to know the illustrious decrees of Heaven? Ha, ha! Let me die now, then! If Blue Bamboo weeps for me, that's all I ask. I have nothing else left to hope for."

Thus our Yü Jung, though supposedly steeped in the Way of the ancient sages, gave in to the depths of his despair and resolved to end his life in the waters of Lake Tung-t'ing. When night fell, a hazy full moon floated up in the sky; the border between the lake and the heavens was lost in a white, misty blur; the wide, flat shore shone as bright as day; the willows along the bank hung heavy with dew; the countless blossoms of a distant plum grove glistened like so many precious gems; and from time to time a faint breeze, like a sigh from heaven, whispered over the sand. A perfectly lovely evening in spring—knowing that this was to be the last he would see of this world, Yü Jung wet his sleeves with tears, and when the melancholy cry of a wild monkey echoed through the night, his sorrow reached the point no man can bear. He was about to plunge into the water when he heard a flutter of wings behind him, and then a melodious voice:

"Long time no see."

Yü Jung turned to see a beautiful woman of twenty or so, with pearl-like teeth and eyes that glistened in the moonlight.

"Who are you?" he said. "Forgive me," he added. "I'm sorry."

"Naughty boy," said the woman, slapping him lightly on the arm. "Don't tell me you've forgotten your Blue Bamboo?"

"Blue Bamboo!"

Yü Jung leaped in astonishment. He hesitated for a moment but then abandoned all reserve and threw his arms around her.

"Let go! I can't breathe!" she said, laughing and slipping deftly out of his embrace. "I'm not going anywhere. From now on I'll be at your side forever."

"Yes! Tell me it's true! I looked for you and couldn't find you, and I was just about to jump in the lake and end it all. Where have you been?"

"Far from here, in Han-yang. After we lost you I left this place, and now I'm a sacred crow of the Han River. An old friend of mine from the shrine came to me this evening to tell me she'd seen you, and I flew here as fast as my wings would carry me. Blue Bamboo is with you now, my love. You mustn't think any more about dying—I simply won't have it. But look at you. You've lost weight."

"I don't wonder. I failed the examination again. There's no telling how they'll treat me at home if I go back now. I'm just so fed up with this life!"

"You suffer because you think the only life you can have is in the place you were born. 'Green hills are where you find them'—isn't that a line from a poem you scholars are always quoting? Come see my house in Han-yang. I'll show you how wonderful it is to be alive."

"But Han-yang is such a long way," said Yü Jung. At some point they had left the balcony of the temple and begun to stroll along the moonlit shore together. "Confucius says: *While his parents are alive, a good son does not wander far afield.*" Ever willing to display some fragment of his virtuous learning, Yü Jung delivered these words with a grave and scholarly look on his face.

"What are you talking about, silly? You're an orphan."

"Oops. You knew that, did you? Still, though, I do have a lot of relatives back home who are the same as parents to me. What I wouldn't give to show them a Yü Jung who's made a great success of himself! They've always treated me as if I were an absolute fool. I know! Rather than going to Han-yang, I'll take you back home with me. Imagine their surprise when they see that beautiful face of yours! That's it, that's what we should do. Come with me. Just once in my life I'd like to stand tall in front of those relatives of mine. To be respected by those back home is the greatest happiness, and the ultimate victory, for any man."

"Why are you so concerned about what the people back home think? 'Fame-seekers'—isn't that what they call those who strive to be respected in their native districts? *Your village fame-seekers are the thieves of virtue*—that's in the *Analects* too, you know."

So crushed was Yü Jung by this stunning rebuttal that he could only bow his head in surrender. "So be it: take me to Han-yang," he said, then tried to hide his embarrassment by reciting a poem. "Those who have passed beyond," he intoned, even as he realized the quote's irrelevance, "take refuge in neither day nor night."

`You'll go?" cried Blue Bamboo. "Oh, I'm so glad! I've already asked my servants to prepare the house for you. Close your eyes for a moment."

Yü Jung obediently let his eyelids droop shut. He heard the flutter of wings again, felt a thin garment fall over his shoulders, and instantly had the sensation of being light and buoyant. When he opened his eyes, both he and Blue Bamboo were crows. Their jet-black feathers gleamed in the moonlight as they hopped along the shore and then spread their wings and left the ground, crying out as if with a single voice.

For hours they flew, swerving and swooping erratically as they followed the winding Yangtze River on its great northeasterly journey, three thousand leagues by the pale light of the moon. When night at last faded to dawn, the tile roofs of the silent, sleeping houses of Han-yang, the city of canals, appeared ahead, shining in morning mist, and now they could see the trees of that fair city, the fragrant, lush green grasses of Parrot Isle, and Yellow Crane Tower and Ch'ing-ch'uan Pagoda murmuring together of days gone by from opposite banks of the brightening stream, where white-sailed boats busily plied the current. Soon they were directly above the lofty peak of Ta-pieh Mountain, at the foot of which lay the vast waters of Moon Lake and beyond which the Han River meandered off to the northern horizon. Confronted with this panoramic view of the Venice of the Orient, Yü Jung remembered Ts'ui Hao's famous poem—"The paths that lead to home, where can they be? These misty waters bring only grief"— and as he dreamily muttered the lines to himself, Blue Bamboo began to circle serenely over a small island in the Han.

"We're home," she called over her shoulder, and he fell in behind her, describing a leisurely circle over the island and looking down to see, amid the luxuriant green river willows bedewed as if with wisps of smoke, a lovely little palace, like a doll's house, from which at that very moment five or six doll-like maidservants came running out, looking up to the sky and waving. Blue Bamboo signaled to Yü Jung with her eyes, furled her wings, and dove headfirst toward the palace, and he followed right behind her. The moment they alighted on the island's green grass they were once again a noble young gentleman and his lovely lady. Surrounded by the maidservants who'd come out to greet them, they smiled at each other, joined hands, and walked to the front door of the charming little palace.

Blue Bamboo led Yü Jung to the palace's innermost chamber. It was dark inside; the gold and silver threads of the curtains glinted dully in the dim, smoky blue light of a single candle. Next to the bed was a small red tray laden with rare wines and delicacies.

"Is it nighttime again already?" Yü Jung asked foolishly.

"Don't tease me like that," said Blue Bamboo, her cheeks reddening as she added, in a softer voice: "I just thought . . . After all, it's our first time together like this, and . . ."

"Ah. Well, Confucius did say that the superior man prefers to conceal his virtue." Yü Jung smiled sheepishly at his own feeble joke. "But then, on the other hand, he also warns us against the folly of 'living in obscurity and practicing wonders.' We should open the curtains and feast our eyes on the famous scenery—Han-yang in spring!"

Yü Jung drew the curtain and flung open the window. Golden morning light poured into the room. Outside, plum trees bloomed in pink profusion, the songs of a hundred bush warblers rippled through the air, and wavelets sparkled in the sun as they splashed and danced over the surface of the river.

"It's so beautiful. How I'd love to show this to my wife back home!"

The words slipped past Yü Jung's lips before he could think to stop them, and he was appalled. Don't tell me you still feel anything for that hideous woman, he berated himself, searching the depths of his heart. And then, suddenly, for reasons he didn't understand, tears welled up in his eyes.

"It appears you can't forget your wife after all," whispered Blue Bamboo, peering at him.

"Don't be silly. That woman hasn't the slightest respect for my learning. She makes me wash the dirty clothes, and push boulders around . . . Besides, they say she's my uncle's mistress. There's nothing about her that's worth remembering."

"Perhaps that's precisely what you find so precious about her, precisely what makes you miss her so—that she's beyond redemption. I'm certain that's what you really feel, deep inside. Didn't Mencius say that compassion lies deep in every man's heart? I think your true and greatest aspiration was to share life's hardships with your wife, to live with her free of malice or resentment or spite, for the rest of your days. Go home." Blue Bamboo's countenance had suddenly taken on a forbidding sternness; she spoke the words sharply and without the least equivocation. "Go now."

Yü Jung was distraught. "How can you say such a thing?" he protested. "You bring me here and try to seduce me, and now you tell me to leave. Who was it that shamed me into forsaking my home in the first place, with all that talk about fame-seekers? You've been toying with my affections all this time!"

"I am a goddess," said Blue Bamboo in an even sterner tone of voice, her eyes fixed on the glittering, flowing waters of the river before her. "You may have failed your government's examination, but you've passed Heaven's test with flying colors. The deity of King Wu Shrine commanded me to investigate you, to test you, to determine whether you honestly envied his crows. Human beings who believe they could find true happiness as a bird or beast are despised by the gods more than any others. To warn you of the error of your ways, you were shot with an arrow and sent back to the human world. But you returned and prayed to become a bird again. This time the deity decided to send you on a long journey and tempt you with carnal pleasures. It was a test to see whether you'd so lose yourself in those pleasures that you'd forget all about your life as a human being. If you had forgotten, the punishment would have been terrible—too terrible for words. Human beings must suffer through their entire lives amid the love and hate that rule their world. There is no escape. All you can do is endure. Endure and struggle, struggle and endure. Learning is a splendid thing, but to make a show of having risen above worldly affairs is cowardly and mean. You must become even more attached to the world, and spend your life immersed in the hardships it presents you with. That's what the gods most love to see in a person. I'm having the servants prepare a boat for you. Get on it, and return directly to your home. Farewell."

The moment she uttered that final word of parting, Blue Bamboo vanished—as did the palace, the garden, and everything else. Mouth agape, Yü Jung stood there all alone on that little isle in the river.

A rudderless, sailless, dugout barge came sliding up to the shore, and Yü Jung boarded it as if in a trance. No sooner had he done so than the barge left the shore and propelled itself down the Han, then up the Yangtze to Lake Tung-t'ing, and across the lake, finally coming to rest at the shore of a fishing village near Yü Jung's home. When he stepped ashore, the unmanned barge pulled away and headed back the way it had come, until it disappeared in the mist.

Yü Jung, disconsolate and numb with dread, peeked timorously through the rear door into the dark interior of his house. Imagine his surprise when a sweet, melodious voice called out, "You're home!" and the woman who rushed, smiling, to greet him turned out to be . . .

"Blue Bamboo!"

"What are you talking about? Where have you been all this time? I got really sick and had a terrible fever, and there was no one to care for me and I missed you so much and realized what a mistake I'd made treating you so badly all this time and, oh, you don't know how I've longed for you to return! The fever just wouldn't go down, and after a while my whole body got all purple and swollen, but I knew it was my punishment for being so mean to a nice person like you, I mean I knew I had it coming, so I just resigned myself to death, but then my skin burst open and all this blue liquid came gushing out and I felt so light and easy, and then this morning I looked in the mirror and my face had changed completely—just look how pretty I am!—and it made me so happy I forgot all about my illness and got out of bed and started cleaning the house like mad, and now here you are! You've come home! I'm so happy! Say you'll forgive me. It's not only my face that's changed, you know—my whole body is different. And my heart too! I'm so sorry for the way I treated you. But all the evil inside me was flushed away with that blue water, honest it was, so please say you'll forget the past and forgive me and let me stay by your side forever!"

A year later a beautiful baby boy was born. Yü Jung named the boy Han-ch'an, which means "child of the Han River," but he never told anyone, not even his beloved wife, why he'd chosen that name. It was a precious secret that he kept buried in his heart, along with the memories of his time as a sacred crow, for the rest of his life. Nor was he ever again heard to utter another pompous word about the "Way of the superior man," but quietly carried on in the same humble poverty as before. And while it's true that he never did earn even a sliver of respect from his relatives, this no longer seemed to bother him in the least. He lived out the rest of his days as a rustic bumpkin of the commonest sort, and buried himself in the dust of the world.

Alt Heidelberg

t was eight years ago. An Imperial University student exceptional only for my laziness, I spent the summer that year at Mishima, on the old Tōkaidō Road. Having managed to wheedle fifty yen from my elder sister, who made it abundantly clear that this was to be the last time, I stuffed an extra yukata and shirt into a schoolbag and breezed out of my boarding house. Had I immediately jumped on a train, all would have been well, but I took a detour and stopped at a pub I frequented in those days. Three friends of mine were there. They were already drunk and demanded to know where I was going all dressed up like that. Caught off guard, I found myself lamely explaining that I wasn't going anywhere special, really, but why didn't they come along? Once that less-than-heartfelt invitation escaped my lips I had no choice but to stick to it, and did so with a reckless vengeance. Look here, I said—fifty yen, I got it from my sister back home, why don't we all take a little trip? Pack? What's wrong with the clothes you've got on? Though I had no idea what would come of this, I refused to be denied and all but dragged them from the pub. I was a child in those days, and a bit of a goof. But the world was gentler then and allowed us to be that way.

The plan was to spend some time in Mishima and write a story. It was there that Takabe Sakichi, who was two years my junior and whose older brother ran a large

95

saké brewery in Numazu, had recently opened a liquor shop. Sakichi and I had met in a casual way and hit it off immediately, perhaps because we were both younger sons and had both lost our fathers at an early age. I had been introduced to his brother and thought him a warm and likeable gentleman, but Sakichi, in spite of the fact that he monopolized the adoration of his entire family, found much to complain of in his role as the number two son. He had once run away from home and shown up smiling at my boarding house in Tokyo, and it was only after a good deal of petulant negotiation with the family that things calmed down somewhat and he took possession of a cozy little home on the outskirts of Mishima, where he now lived with his twenty-year-old sister and stocked casks of his brother's saké for retail sale. This was the house I planned to go to. Sakichi had described the place to me in a letter, but I had yet to visit him there. I intended to go to Mishima and see if things looked promising; if they didn't I'd return at once, and if they did I'd spend the summer there and write my story.

Now, however, against my better judgment, I'd gone and invited my three friends. I bought four tickets for Mishima and herded them aboard the train, feigning confidence but inwardly wondering if it was right to impose this mob on Sakichi at his little home. As the train rolled on, my anxiety only increased, and by the time night had fallen and we were nearing Mishima Station, my misgivings had so overwhelmed me that I literally began to tremble, and tears welled up in my eyes. I didn't want my friends to sense my panic, however, and concentrated on telling them what a great fellow Sakichi was. "Once we get to Mishima, we'll have it made," I said again and again, repeating this idiotic and meaningless formula so many times it made even me sick. I'd sent a telegram to Sakichi beforehand, but would he actually be there to meet us? What would I do with my three friends if he didn't show? I'd lose all face, my honor would be stained forever.

When we got off at Mishima Station and filed out through the gate, there wasn't a soul in sight. My worst fear had been realized, and I had to suppress a whimper. From the station, situated in the middle of open fields, one couldn't even see the lights of town. It was pitch dark whichever direction I looked, and the only sounds were the sigh of the wind over rice paddies and a heart-piercing chorus of frogs. I was at a complete loss as to what to do. Without Sakichi, there was simply no way I could handle this situation. What with the train fare and this and that, the fifty yen I'd received from my sister was nearly exhausted. I knew my friends had no money, of course, and I'd been fully aware of that when I dragged them from the restaurant. They seemed to have implicit confidence in me, however, which left me in the difficult position of having to pretend that everything was under control. I forced a smile and spoke out in a loud voice.

"That's Sakichi for you—irresponsible as ever. He must have forgotten what time I said I was arriving. We'll have to walk—there aren't any buses or anything." I said this as if I knew the place well, then picked up my bag and had just begun to march off, when a pair of yellow headlights appeared out of the darkness, bouncing toward us.

"Ah! It's a bus!" I said. "I, ah, I guess they have buses now." Thoroughly braced, I commanded my troops to line up behind me at the side of the road, and there we awaited the slowly lumbering vehicle. When it finally came to a stop in front of the station, Sakichi, cool and composed in a white yukata, was among the passengers who filed out. I all but groaned with relief.

Sakichi's arrival was my salvation. He took us by hired car to Kona Hot Springs, where we stayed at the finest inn and ate and drank to the point of stupefaction. The following day my friends headed back to Tokyo, raucously thanking me for showing them such a good time. Due to Sakichi's mediation, we'd been given a special rate at the inn, and I was able to cover it all, but after I'd bought the return tickets for my friends I had less than half a yen left.

"Sakichi," I said, "I'm broke. Is there a room in your house I can sleep in?"

Sakichi said nothing, only slapped me on the back. And thus began my summer at his house in Mishima.

Mishima was a beautiful place, one that time had passed by. Spider-webbing the entire town was a rushing network of crystal-clear streams, the beds of which were green with waterplants. These streams flowed through the gardens of all the homes, dipped under verandas, and babbled along beside kitchen doors, so that people could wash their clothes in fresh, clean water without ever leaving their houses. Long ago the town had been a famous stop on the Tōkaidō Road, but its fortunes had gradually declined, and now only the old-timers clung with stubborn pride to the flashy manners and customs of livelier, more prosperous days—abandoning themselves, if you will, to the dignified vagrancy of a dying breed.

From time to time a flea market was held in a lot behind Sakichi's house, and I once went to see it but ended up wanting to cover my eyes. They'd try to sell you anything. Seeing a man sell the bicycle he'd arrived on was strange enough, but nothing compared to the old fellow who pulled a used harmonica out of his pocket and parted with it for five sen. An old scroll with a painting of Bodhidharma, a silver-plated watch chain, a woman's coat with a soiled collar, a toy train, mosquito netting, homemade paintings, *go* stones, a carpenter's plane, swaddling clothes—without so much as cracking a smile, buyers and sellers haggled over these treasures, trying to beat each other out of three or four sen. Most of the people who'd gathered were older men, in their forties or fifties or even sixties, and I imagined that they'd come to this after lives of dissipation; now, for want of a quart of unrefined saké, they kicked or shoved aside their tearful, pleading wives and children as they carried away the last object of any value left in the house—or "borrowed" the grandchild's harmonica, then slipped out the back door and scurried down to the flea market. One elderly fellow was selling his prayer beads for two sen. Even more outrageous was a bald retiree who showed up with the remains of a woman's lined kimono wadded in a ball and stuffed in his pocket. It was filthy and falling apart—no longer what you could call a piece of clothing—and with barely contained desperation and a sneer of self-contempt, he spread these rags out on the ground and asked for bids.

The town itself was in a severe state of decay. We'd go out to drink at a run-down old joint that had been an inn long ago, with low-hanging eaves and oil-paper sliding doors, and the ancient shopkeeper there would insist on warming our saké himself. He proudly stated that he'd been heating saké for his customers for half a century and insisted that the taste of rice wine depended entirely on the way it was warmed. If he was typical of the older generation, you can imagine what the young men were like:

slender, dashing rogues devoted to play and pleasure. A number of them, loafers and ruffians of every description, would gather each morning at Sakichi's shop. Though Sakichi didn't appear to be particularly strong, perhaps he was in fact a formidable brawler; all these fellows seemed to look up to him. I'd be on the second floor, writing, while the morning assembly began downstairs, and suddenly I'd hear Sakichi's voice rising above the general clamor.

"Hell, that's nothing compared to the fellow staying upstairs here. You could scour the entire Ginza in Tokyo without finding a man like him. Can he fight? Phew! He's been in jail, you know. Expert at karate too. Look at this pillar. You see how it's caved in here? He did that with his fist."

None of which, needless to say, contained a speck of truth. Distressed, I'd shuffle downstairs, call Sakichi over, and speak to him in a low voice, pursing my lips in disapproval.

"Don't be saying crazy things like that. I won't be able to show my face around here."

Sakichi would smile and say: "Nobody takes it seriously. They know I'm making it up as I go. As long as the story's interesting, they're happy."

"Is that so? Regular lovers of the arts, eh? But listen, no more lies like that, all right? You're making me nervous." And with that, I'd go back up to the second floor and resume work on my story, which I'd entitled "Romanesque." Before long, however, I'd hear Sakichi's booming voice again.

"Talk about holding your liquor, there's nobody who can touch the fellow upstairs. Every evening he drinks a quart of saké, and all that does is make his cheeks a little rosy. Then he stands up, real casual, and says, 'Hey, Sakichi—let's go to the baths.' After a quart of saké, mind you. At the baths, he whips out an old Japanese razor and shaves, nothing to it. Not so much as a nick. Sometimes he even shaves *my* beard. Then, as soon as we get home, he goes right back to work. Cool as a cucumber."

This too was a series of lies. Every evening, whether I asked for it or not, a half-pint bottle of saké would be on my dinner tray. Not wanting to appear ungrateful, I'd guzzle it down quickly enough, but it was, remember, saké delivered directly from the brewery, not at all diluted, and therefore extremely potent. On one bottle you'd get as drunk as you normally would on two or three. Sakichi didn't drink the saké from his family's brewery, claiming it would make him gag to think of the inflated profit his brother turned on the stuff, and so whenever he wanted to drink, he went elsewhere. I, therefore, unseemly though it may have been, would get drunk alone at dinner, draining my bottle of saké and then, as my head began to swim, digging into the food; and no sooner would I finish eating than Sakichi would invite me to the baths. Not wanting to seem selfish by asking to be allowed to rest awhile first, I always accepted, and off we'd go. In the baths I'd feel as if I were going to faint, or die. I'd stagger toward the dressing room to make my escape, but Sakichi would stop me, tell me I needed a shave, and kindly offer to give me one, and again I'd find myself unable to refuse, surrendering with a lame, "Well, if you really don't mind . . ." Utterly exhausted by the time it was all over, I'd wobble home, mutter something about doing a little more work, crawl upstairs, collapse on the floor, and fall fast asleep. Surely

Sakichi was aware of all this, and I'll never know why he insisted on telling those preposterous yarns.

The yearly festival of the famous Grand Shrine of Mishima was fast approaching. The young ruffians who gathered at Sakichi's shop were all members of the festival committee, and each day they excitedly hashed out their various plans and ideas—dancing platforms, parades, floats, fireworks, what have you. I was told that Mishima's fireworks display boasted a long tradition and included a special event in which fireworks were set up in the shrine's pond so that, reflected on the water, they appeared to come bubbling up from the depths. Large, printed programs listing the names of some hundred different fireworks to be launched were distributed to all the houses, and with each passing day the festival spirit began to infuse the town with a strangely poignant, pulsating buoyancy.

On the morning of the day of the festival the weather was fine. When I went out to the well to wash my face, Sakichi's younger sister took the kerchief from her head, bowed deeply, and said, "Congratulations," and I surprised myself by returning this traditional festival greeting with minimal awkwardness. I found Sakichi dressed in everyday clothes and maintaining an aloof attitude as he puttered about in his shop. When the usual gang began to arrive dressed in gaudy yukata with the same wave-shaped pattern, festival fans stuck in their sashes and matching hand towels draped around their necks, they all offered us their congratulations on the day. I'd felt rather restless since waking up that morning but didn't have it in me to join the youths in pulling the floats through the streets, so I went upstairs and sat down to do a bit of work. Soon, however, I was back on my feet, pacing the room. I leaned on the window sill and looked down into the garden, where in the shade of a fig tree Sakichi's sister was washing our clothes as if it were just another ordinary day.

"Sai-chan!" I shouted down to her. "You should be at the festival!"

"I hate watching men strut around!" she shouted back, and went on with her scrubbing. "It's like when an alcoholic walks by a liquor shop," she added in a normal tone of voice. "It makes me shiver all over." I could tell she was laughing by the way her squarish shoulders jiggled. Though she was only twenty, the sister seemed more mature than Sakichi, who was twenty-two, or myself for that matter, her elder by four years. She had a healthy, energetic way about her and virtually acted as guardian to Sakichi and me.

Sakichi too displayed an irritable edginess that day. Though he would have liked to enjoy himself frolicking about with the boys, his pride positively forbade him to don a gaudy wave-pattern yukata, and he reacted by taking a particularly cynical view of the whole affair. "Ah, what a load of rot this is," he said. "I'm closing the store for the day. We're not selling saké to anyone!" And with that he got on his bicycle and rode off. Shortly afterward I received a telephone call from him, telling me to come join him at the usual place. I changed into my clean yukata and flew out of the house, feeling as if I'd been rescued. The "usual place" was the shop with the old man who was so proud of having warmed saké for fifty years. I found Sakichi and another young man named Ejima there, drinking grimly. I had drunk with Ejima two or three times before. He, like Sakichi, was the disaffected son of a wealthy family, and as far as I could tell he did nothing each day but seethe with anger toward the world. He was every bit as handsome as Sakichi, who you must know possessed what could only be called a beautiful face. And, sure enough, Ejima too took a dim view of the festival and was expressing his defiance by deliberately putting on his shabbiest everyday clothes and hunkering down in this dark shop, sipping at his saké as if it were poison. I joined them, and we sat drinking in silence for some time; but outside it was growing ever noisier, with throngs of people clumping by, firecrackers going off, and sellers loudly hawking their wares, until Ejima, apparently unable to bear it another moment, stood up abruptly. "Come on. Let's go to the river," he said, and strode out of the shop without even waiting to hear our response.

The three of us tramped through the town, intentionally choosing back streets, each of us casting meaningless aspersions on the festival. ("Shit. Just listen to those idiots!") We were soon outside the town limits, heading in the direction of Numazu, and by sundown we'd reached Ejima's summer home on the bank of the Kano River. We went in through the back door and discovered an elderly man, clad only in a shirt, in the drawing room.

Ejima shouted at him: "What the hell? How long you been here? Out gambling all night again, were you? Leave us. Go home. I brought some guests."

The old man scrambled to his feet and briefly flashed us a courteous smile, whereupon Sakichi bowed so deeply and respectfully that I was startled.

"You'd better put something on," Ejima said indifferently, "or you'll catch a cold. Oh, and before you leave, call up and have some beer delivered, and something to eat.

The festival's a bore, so we're going to sit here and drink ourselves blind."

"Very well, my lord," the old man waggishly replied. He draped himself in his kimono and trotted off, and no sooner was he gone than Sakichi burst out laughing and said: "That's Ejima's father. He thinks his son is heaven's gift to the world. 'Very well, my lord'—did you hear that?"

Before long the beer arrived, along with a variety of tasty dishes, and I remember us at some point harmonizing on a lyric I couldn't make any sense of whatsoever. Blanketed in the evening haze, the swollen river before us flowed leisurely along, lapping the green leaves on either bank. Its waters were a deep and astounding shade of blue, and, apropos of absolutely nothing, I found myself thinking that this must be what the Rhine looked like.

When the beer ran out, we headed back to Mishima. It was quite a long hike, and even as I shuffled along I nodded and nearly dozed off any number of times. Catching myself, I'd open my eyes a slit and see a firefly zip past my brow. When we got back to Sakichi's house, his mother was there, having come from Numazu for a visit. I excused myself, went upstairs, hung my mosquito netting, and went to sleep, only to awaken shortly to the sound of loud voices. I looked out the window and saw that a ladder had been propped up against the eaves. Sakichi and his mother were on the ground at the foot of the ladder, engaged in a beautiful dispute.

For the finale of the fireworks display, they were going to send up the "two-footer," a rocket two feet in diameter that had for days been the topic of excited discussion among the young people in town. It was almost time for the two-footer to be launched. Sakichi intended to have his mother see it, and wasn't going to take no for an answer. He was still quite drunk.

"I wanna show it to you—what, you don't wanna see it? We'll have a good view on the roof . . . I told you, I'll *carry* you up there. All you gotta do is grab hold of me!"

His mother was balking at the idea. I saw the sister there, too, her outline pale in the dim light, and she seemed to be chuckling to herself. Though no one else was around, the mother looked about timidly, then finally sealed her resolve and climbed on Sakichi's back.

"All right. Up we go!" The mother was about sixty, and definitely on the plump side. Sakichi didn't seem to be having an easy time of it.

"No problem, no problem," he said, slowly pulling himself up the first rungs of the ladder. I watched them and thought: That's it. That's why Sakichi's mother is so devoted to him. That's why, however selfish and reckless his way of life, she's willing to defend him even if it means pitting herself against her eldest son. I went back to bed contented, feeling I'd seen something better than a two-foot skyrocket.

I have many other vivid memories of Mishima, but I'll save them for some other time. "Romanesque," the piece I wrote that summer, was praised by a few people, and it has been my fate ever since, in spite of an utter lack of belief in myself, to carry on with my clumsy attempts at writing. Mishima is a place I'll never forget. The impact that summer had on my life was such that it would scarcely be an exaggeration to say that all the work I've done since has been the result of what I learned there.

Now, eight years later, it's no longer possible for me to wheedle money from my sister; I'm out of touch with my family and am merely another undernourished, impoverished writer. Recently, having finally come into a fair amount of ready cash, I took an overnight trip to Izu with my wife and her mother and younger sister. We got off the train at Shimizu, visited Miho and Shuzenji, and the following day, on the way home, we stopped at Mishima. It's a great place, a really great place, I kept telling the ladies as I whisked them off the train, and while I showed them about the town I tried to work myself into high spirits, recounting my memories of Mishima as amusingly as I could but gradually growing more and more crestfallen and finally slipping into such a funk that I completely lost the will to speak. The Mishima before my eyes was a desolate place, inhabited by strangers. Sakichi and his sister were no longer there. Ejima probably wasn't either. The youths who'd once assembled each day at Sakichi's shop were undoubtedly at home, yelling at their wives with sour, know-it-all looks on their faces. I couldn't find a trace of the old atmosphere anywhere. But perhaps it wasn't that Mishima's colors had faded but simply that my own heart had grown old and withered. That carefree Imperial University student has since had eight solid years of trial and tribulation. I've aged a good two decades in those eight years.

As if things weren't bad enough, it began to rain. My wife and her mother and sister did their best to praise the town, saying it was nice and quiet and relaxed, but their faces betrayed their perplexity and discomfort. Exasperated, I guided them to the drinking shop I'd once frequented. The building was so filthy that the women hesitated before passing through the gate, but I insisted, raising my voice in spite of myself, saying: "It's a foul-looking place, but the saké's good. There's an old man here who's spent the better part of a century doing nothing but heating up saké. This shop's a legend in Mishima." Once we were inside, however, I saw that the old man in the red shirt was no longer there. An insipid-looking waitress came out and took our order. The tables and benches were the same as before, but an electric phonograph occupied one corner of the shop, a large poster featuring a vulgar illustration of a movie actress hung on the wall, and the atmosphere was thick with decline. Hoping to sweep away the gloom by at least bringing a festive mood to the table, I ordered an extravagant spread.

"We'll have broiled eel, grilled prawns, and egg custard, four of each. If you can't prepare it here, send out for it. And bring us some saké."

My mother-in-law, beside me, was fidgeting. "We don't need all that," she said. "It'll just go to waste." There was no way I could have explained the anguish in my heart, and that only made it all the more unbearable. I've never felt more depressed in my life.

ROMANESQUE

TARŌ THE WIZARD

nce upon a time, in the village of Kanagi in Tsugaru Province, there lived a country squire by the name of Kuwagata Sōsuke. Sōsuke was forty-nine before he was blessed with his first child, a son whom he named Tarō. No sooner had Tarō come into the world than he spread his jaws in a yawn, the prodigious size of which so tormented Sōsuke that when relatives came to offer their congratulations he was unable even to look them in the eye. Sōsuke's fears were soon to prove warranted. Upon waking in the morning, Tarō never crawled eagerly out of bed but would lie there with his eyes closed for an extra hour or two, pretending to be asleep; held in the folds of his mother's kimono, he wouldn't bother to seek out her breast but would merely let his mouth hang open and wearily wait for the nipple to brush against his lips; and when he was given a swivel-necked papier-mâché tiger with which to amuse himself, he made no effort to play with the toy but only gazed listlessly at its comically bobbing head. He was, in short, a child whose nature it was to despise any sort of unnecessary exertion. And yet, when he was three years old, Tarō was responsible for a little incident that lent his name considerable notoriety among the people of the village. It was by no means an incident of the sort that gets written up in newspapers; you may rest assured, therefore,

111

that it really happened. Tarō went for a walk . . . and just kept walking.

It was a night in early spring. Tarō slipped silently from his mother's embrace, tumbled out of bed, rolled to the dirt floor of the entrance hall, and continued rolling, right out the door. Once outside, he climbed to his feet. Sōsuke and his wife, meanwhile, slept on unaware.

A mist-blurred full moon hung low in the sky, just inches above Tarō's forehead. Barefoot and dressed in an underkimono with a killifish motif and a padded cotton vest with a pattern of arrowhead roots, he headed east along the horsedung-littered road. He walked with his sleepy eyes half-closed, breathing in short, hurried little huffs and puffs.

The next morning the village was in an uproar. Tarō had been found sleeping innocently in the middle of an apple orchard on Rolling Springs Mountain, more than two miles from the village. Rolling Springs Mountain was shaped like a half-melted block of ice. The peak consisted of three softly curved undulations, and the western side formed a gentle slope that resembled water flowing. The reason Tarō had ended up atop a three-hundred-foot mountain wasn't clear. There was no doubt that he'd gone alone. But no one could figure out why.

He was discovered by a young woman who'd been out gathering ferns. She placed him in her basket and carried him, gently rocking from side to side, back to the village. Those villagers who came up to peer into the basket, creasing their brows with dark, greasy wrinkles, whispered of goblins and nodded to one another knowingly.

When Sōsuke saw his son home safe and sound, all he could say was: "Well, well." He didn't say he was upset and didn't say he was relieved. Tarō's mother, for her part, scarcely seemed agitated at all. She lifted Tarō from the girl's basket, replacing him with a roll of cotton toweling as a reward, then set a large tub on the dirt floor of the entrance hall, filled it to the brim with hot water, and calmly began to bathe the boy. Not that Tarō was the least bit dirty; his naked body was plump and round and white. Sōsuke paced back and forth restlessly beside the tub until at last he tripped against it and sent water splashing over the floor from wall to wall. Though his wife scolded him for this in a shrill and angry voice, he remained where he was, peeking over her shoulder at Taro's face and saying, again and again: "Tarō, what did you see? What did you see, Tarō?" Tarō, after yawning any number of times, shouted in a broken babble: *"Peebo stobuu, beezee buunee."*

It wasn't until late that night, as Sōsuke lay in bed, that he finally perceived the meaning of these words. They were from Emperor Nintoku's famous poem: "Climbing the palace tower / I see smoke fill the air / *The people's stoves are busily burning.*" Such was the impact of this realization that Sōsuke reflexively tried to slap his knee, and might have succeeded had he not been hindered by the heavy quilts; as it was, he ended up striking himself, quite painfully, on the bellybutton. The son of a squire, he reflected, is the father of a squire. At the age of three the boy is already concerned for the people's welfare. Ah—a blessed ray of hope! No doubt Tarō had gazed down from Rolling Springs Mountain upon Kanagi Village awaking in the dawn and envisioned the chimneys of all the houses sending up prosperous billows of smoke as the people cooked their morning meals. By heaven, it's the pious wish of a noble, lofty soul. What a godsend this child is! I must take special care of him. Sōsuke sat up quietly, reached over to where Tarō was sleeping between him and his wife, and carefully rearranged the quilts. Then, stretching even farther, he did the same for his wife, albeit somewhat less carefully. The wife wasn't pleasant to look at when she slept; Sōsuke turned his head sternly to one side and muttered to himself as he tugged at her bedding: "This is the woman who gave birth to Tarō. I must take good care of her too."

Tarō's babbled words proved prophetic. That spring, all the apple orchards in the village burst into bloom with oversized rouge blossoms whose fragrance wafted as far as the castle town, some twenty-five miles away. Autumn brought even better things: apples as big as grapefruit and as red as coral hung from the trees in dense clusters. So juicy were these apples that if you plucked one and bit into it, the skin would burst with a loud crack, and sweet, cold spray would gush out to soak your nose and cheeks. On New Year's Day the following year, an auspicious event occurred: a thousand cranes appeared from out of the east. The entire village came out to point and gasp as the cranes slowly circled overhead in the blue New Year's sky and finally soared off to the west. That fall, too, at harvest time, the ears of rice produced ears of rice and the boughs of the apple trees bent low with the weight of clusters of fruit every bit as wonderful as the previous year's. The village began to prosper. Sōsuke was convinced that it was all because of his son's prophetic powers, but he refrained from telling the villagers this. Perhaps he didn't want to be sneered at for being a blindly doting father. Or—who knows?—perhaps he had some vague ulterior motive and hoped to use Tarō's gift to line his own pockets.

Sadly, however, after two or three years, the infant prodigy began to stray from the path of virtue. At some point the villagers took to referring to him as "Tarō the Lazy," and even Sōsuke had to admit that it was only to be expected. At six and seven years of age Tarō never went out to the fields and paddies and riverbanks to play as other children did; in summer he'd sit at the window ledge with his chin on his hand and gaze at the scenery outside, and in winter he'd lie by the hearth and stare at the firewood going up in flames. He seemed to take pleasure only in riddles. One winter night, as he lay in a heap by the fire, he squinted up at the face of Sōsuke beside him and drawled: "What is it . . . that can fall in the water . . . without getting wet?" Sōsuke slowly swiveled his head to the left, then to the right, then back again, as he pondered. "I don't know," he said at last. Tarō let his eyelids droop shut before giving the answer: "A shadow." Sōsuke was more vexed with his son at that moment than ever before. This child is a moron, he thought. No doubt about it—he's an idiot. A worthless lazybones, just as the villagers say.

And so it went until the autumn of Tarō's tenth year, when the village was devastated by a flood. Kanagi River, normally a stream no more than five yards across that flowed lazily along the northern edge of the village, was driven to a mad rage by a month of steadily falling rain. The muddy headwaters swelled, forming whirlpools great and small, and the six branches of the river merged to rush down the mountain at a furious speed, sweeping away hundreds of freshly cut logs, uprooting the oaks and firs and poplars that grew on the banks and hurling them downstream, gathering in a great pool at the foot of the mountain and then overflowing in one mighty upheaval to smash against the village bridge, demolishing it as if it were made of straw, crashing through the embankments, and spreading out like a vast sea that licked at the walls of all the houses and set the pigs to swimming and the ten thousand sheaves of newly harvested rice to floating upon its rolling waves. It was five days before the rain stopped; ten days later the waters began to recede, and, twenty days after that, Kanagi River was once again a leisurely little stream flowing along the northern border of the village.

The villagers gathered each night in one house or another to discuss what was to be done, and the conclusion was always the same: Sure don't fancy starvin' to death! This consensus was always the starting point of the following night's discussion, during which many questions would be raised but only one conclusion reached: Sure don't fancy starvin' to death! They were making no progress at all and beginning to panic when at last a valiant, public-spirited soul stepped forward. Ten-year-old Tarō turned one day to his father, Sōsuke, who sat with his head cradled in his arms, sighing, and ventured an opinion: "Seems to me there's a simple solution. Someone should go to the castle and ask the daimyo to send emergency relief. I volunteer." It was like a bolt of lightning; Sōsuke shot up in his seat and let out a joyful shout. The shout ended in another sigh of despair, however, as he realized what a rash suggestion this was. He frowned and buried his head in his arms again. "It may sound simple to a child like you, but an adult would know better. Make a direct appeal to the daimyo and it could cost you your life. It's out of the question. Forget it. Don't even consider it." That night, however, Tarō strolled casually out of the house and then, unbeknownst to anyone, hurried straight for the castle town.

Luck was with him. The direct appeal was a success. Far from demanding Tarō's head, the daimyo actually bestowed a reward upon him. It may have been that the daimyo of that time had grown a bit senile and neatly forgotten the laws of the land, but, in any case, thanks to Tarō, the village was saved from extinction. And the following year it began to prosper once again.

For two or three years afterward, the villagers spoke well of Tarō. In time, however, they completely forgot their debt of gratitude and came up with a new name for him: "the squire's idiot son." He spent almost every day in the storehouse, reading at random the books in his father's library. From time to time he came across volumes full of indecent pictures, but these, too, he merely leafed through with an indifferent look on his face.

At some point, however, he discovered a book on wizardry, and this he read with great fervor, devouring it from cover to cover and memorizing every word. After a year of study and practice he acquired the ability to transform himself variously into a mouse, an eagle, and a snake. Casting the spell that made him a mouse, he'd dash about inside the storehouse, stopping every now and then to let out a squeak; as an eagle, he'd spread his wings, fly out the window, and soar through the sky to his heart's content; and in the form of a snake, he'd crawl under the storehouse floor, dodging the cobwebs, and slide through the cool, shadowy weeds on his scaly belly. Before long he learned how to turn himself into a praying mantis as well, but this proved disappointing. There was nothing particularly fun about being a praying mantis.

Sōsuke had by now given up on his son entirely. Reluctant to admit defeat, however, he would sometimes turn to his wife and say: "The boy was simply too gifted, that's all."

At sixteen Tarō fell in love. The girl, who was the daughter of the oil-seller next door, was a marvelously skilled flutist. Tarō loved to sit in the storehouse in the form of a mouse or a snake and listen to her play. Ah, he would think, to have that maiden fall in love with me! If only I were the handsomest man in the province! At last it occurred to him to concentrate his wizardly powers on attaining this goal. Discovering an incantation that might help him become handsome, he pronounced it again and again, day after day, and on the tenth day succeeded in casting the spell.

Tarō approached the mirror with his heart in his throat . . . and received the shock of a lifetime. His skin was so white as to be almost colorless; his cheeks were full and round and soft and smooth; his eyes were the narrowest conceivable slits; and a long, stringy mustache drooped down to below his chin. It was a face that would have looked right at home on any eighth-century Buddhist statue. And even the splendid article between his legs resembled those of the men of old, hanging down long and fat and heavy. Imagine Tarō's chagrin when he realized what had happened: The wizardry book was too old; it had been written during the Tempyō era and was hopelessly out of date. I'm not going to get anywhere looking like this, he thought, and decided to start all over. When he tried to undo the spell, however, he discovered that it could not be undone. Apparently if a wizard uses his magic to satisfy his own selfish desires, he's stuck with the result, for better or worse. For three days, four days straight,

ROMANESQUE

Tarō expended his efforts in vain, and on the fifth day he resigned himself. The girl next door was scarcely likely to find him attractive now, but the world was wide and surely not devoid of women with eccentric tastes. Tarō, stripped of his wizardly powers, stepped out of the storehouse with his round, plump cheeks and long, stringy mustache.

After explaining everything to his parents, who stared at him with mouths agape, he finally convinced them to accept what had happened and to close their mouths. That night, leaving only a note that said "Gone on a journey," he left the house abruptly. A full moon hung in the sky. The outline of the moon looked a bit blurred, but it wasn't because of mist; it was because his eyes were so narrow.

Ambling aimlessly along, Tarō reflected upon the riddle of good looks. Why should a face that would have been handsome long ago seem so ridiculous now? It just didn't make sense. What was wrong with the way he looked? This was an awfully difficult riddle, however, and though Tarō pondered it as he passed through the woods outside the neighboring village, as he made his way to the castle town, and even as he crossed the border out of Tsugaru, he was still nowhere near coming up with an answer.

Incidentally, it's said that the secret to Tarō's wizardry involved leaning languidly against a pillar or fence with folded arms and muttering the incantation, "What a bore, what a bore, what a bore," again and again, hundreds of times, until he entered a state of egolessness.

JIRŌBEI THE FIGHTER

nce upon a time, in the town of Mishima, a stopover point on the Tōkaidō Road, there lived a man by the name of Shikamaya Ippei. Ippei's family had been in the business of brewing saké since his great-grandfather's generation. It's said that saké reflects the personality of the brewer, and Ippei's saké, which was called Waterwheel, was crystal clear and extremely dry. Ippei had fourteen children—six boys and eight girls. The eldest son was rather slow when it came to understanding the ways of the world, as a result of which he did just as Ippei told him and put the family business before all other things in life. Though he had no confidence in his own ideas, the eldest son would occasionally hazard an opinion in his father's presence. His courage would fail him even as he spoke, however, and he'd end up retracting his own argument, saying things like: "At least, such would appear to be the case, but then again, one can only conclude that this line of thought is riddled with misconceptions, and I'm sure it's quite wrong, but what do you think, Father? It somehow seems to me I've got it all wrong." To which Ippei would issue a terse reply: "You've got it all wrong."

Matters were a bit different for the second son, Jirōbei. There was in his nature a tendency to display a taste for fairness and justice—not the "fairness and justice" that politicians are forever carrying on about, but fairness and justice in the true, original sense of the words. As a consequence, the people of Mishima regarded him as a troublemaker and kept their distance.

Jirōbei disliked what is known as the tradesman spirit. The world, he maintained, wasn't an abacus. Convinced that the only things of true worth were those without any monetary value whatsoever, he spent most of his days drinking. He refused to drink the saké his family brewed, however, having seen with his own eyes the excessive profit they turned on the stuff. In fact, if he discovered that he'd inadvertently drained a cup of Waterwheel, he would promptly stick a finger down his throat and force it back up. Day after day Jirōbei wandered about the town drinking, but his father, Ippei, never reproached him for it. Ippei was a clearheaded fellow, and it pleased him that at least one of his many children had turned out to be a ne'er-do-well: it lent color to the group. He was also the head of the Mishima fire brigade, an honorary post to which he hoped one day to have Jirōbei succeed him. Farsighted man that he was, Ippei held that if his son were to continue to gallivant about like a wild horse, it would only help him to accumulate the qualifications required of the future head of the fire brigade, and he turned a blind eye to his second son's scandalous behavior.

In the summer of his twenty-second year, Jirōbei decided that, come what may, he was going to make himself into a formidable fighter. There was a reason for this.

On August 15 every year a festival was held at the Great Shrine of Mishima, and tens of thousands of people—not only the townsfolk, but residents of the surrounding mountains and nearby fishing villages—would gather there, all with colorful festival fans stuck in their sashes. For longer than anyone could remember, it had always rained on the day of the festival. Mishima people have a taste for flamboyance, however, and would stand in the rain flapping their fans, drenched to the skin and clenching their teeth to endure the cold as they watched the wheeled dancing platforms and floats passing by and marveled at the fireworks display.

The day of the festival the year Jirōbei turned twenty-two dawned fair and sunny. A single black-eared kite flitted about above the town, lifting its voice in song, and the people who came to the shrine to worship offered thanks first to the god of the shrine and then to the kite and the clear blue sky. It was a little past noon when black clouds suddenly billowed up on the northeastern horizon, and in a matter of seconds a shadow had fallen over Mishima and a moist, heavy wind was crawling and swirling through the streets. Moments later, as if summoned by that wind, large drops of water began to spill from the heavens, and finally the rain, unable to contain itself any longer, poured down in a great torrent.

Jirōbei was drinking saké in a shop across from the gate of the Great Shrine, watching the girls outside running for shelter with little mincing steps, when suddenly he rose up in his seat. He had spotted someone he knew—the daughter of the calligraphy teacher who lived across the street from him. Dressed in a heavy red kimono with a floral pattern, she ran five or six steps, slowed to a walk, ran five or six steps, then slowed to a walk again. Jirōbei dashed outside, parting the shop-curtain that hung at the entrance, and spoke to the girl, saying: "Let me get you an umbrella. You don't want to ruin that nice kimono."

The girl stopped and slowly twisted her slender neck to look at him. When she saw who it was, a blush spread over her soft white cheeks. "Wait one second," Jirōbei said and, ducking back inside, bullied the shopkeeper into lending him a rough, oil-paper umbrella. Ha, calligraphy teacher's daughter! No doubt your old man, your old lady, and you yourself think I'm a good-for-nothing, a drunk, a rogue, and a scoundrel. Well, you've got another think coming. I'm the sort of man who, if I feel sorry for somebody, I'll see to it that they get an umbrella, like this, or anything else they might need. How does that grab you? Jirōbei was inwardly shouting this challenge as he headed back to the street. When he flipped the shop-curtain aside again, however, the girl was gone; there was nothing but the rain, pouring down even harder now, and a stream of people shoving and jostling one another as they ran past. A chorus of catcalls—*Woo! Woo!*—came from inside the shop, where six or seven local toughs were drinking. Jirōbei stood there dangling the umbrella in his right hand and thinking: When you find yourself looking ridiculous, reasoning isn't worth a damn. If a man offends you, strike him down. If a horse offends you, strike it down. That's the way to be, he told himself. And from that day on, for the next three years, Jirōbei stealthily trained in the art of fighting.

What fighting requires, first and foremost, is courage. Jirōbei cultivated his with saké. He was drinking more than ever now. His eyes grew as cold and cloudy as those of a dead fish, and his forehead developed three greasy furrows, which only added to the brazen insolence of his features. His movements became ponderous and deliberate, so that just to lift his pipe to his lips for a single puff he would swing his arm around from behind in a great, sweeping, slow-motion arc. As far as appearances went, at least, he seemed a man with nerves of steel.

Next was the manner of speaking. He decided to speak in a fathomless kind of murmur. Before fighting, of course, it's customary to recite some sort of cocky, clever-sounding threat, and Jirōbei agonized over his choice of words. Clichés rang hollow; at length he settled upon something original: "Aren't you making a bit of a mistake? Or perhaps you're joking. You'd look awfully funny with the tip of your nose all purple and swollen. It would take a hundred days to return to normal. I do think you're making a mistake." In order to be able to deliver these lines smoothly at any given moment, he recited them thirty times each night after going to bed. And as he recited the words, he remembered to refrain from sneering or glaring any more than necessary—maintaining, if anything, a hint of a smile on his lips.

Now he was ready to begin the actual training. Jirōbei was opposed to carrying weapons. Winning a fight with weapons didn't make you a man; if he couldn't gain victory with his bare hands, it just wouldn't feel right. He began his research with the study of how to form a fist. It occurred to him that leaving the thumb outside the fist, unprotected, could result in a sprain. After experimenting with various methods, he tucked his thumb inside and covered it with the knuckles of the other four fingers. This made for a wonderfully hard fist, and when he struck himself on the kneecap with it his hand didn't hurt at all; he felt such pain in his knee, however, that he nearly keeled over. This was a tremendous breakthrough. Next, he set out to make the skin of his knuckles as thick and hard as possible. Each morning when he awoke he clenched his

fist in the manner he'd discovered and punched the hard-
wood tobacco tray next to his pillow. Walking about the
streets of the town, he lashed out at all the stone walls and
wooden fences he passed. He pounded the table at the shop
where he drank, and pummeled the cast-iron hearth in his
house. He spent a year on this stage of the training, and
by the time his tobacco tray was falling to pieces, all the
walls and fences in sight were riddled with holes of various sizes, the table at the drinking shop had developed an
enormous crack, and the hearth in his house was covered
with an almost fashionable pattern of dents and bumps,
Jirōbei was finally sure of the hardness of his fists. He had
also discovered during this stage of the training the secret
to throwing a punch. Punching straight out, piston-like,
was about three times as effective as swinging from the
side, he found. And it was about four times as effective if
you rotated your arm one hundred eighty degrees as you
punched. The fist would dig into your opponent's body like
the tip of a screw.

The following year he trained in the pine forest behind
his house, the site of the former Kokubun Temple. There
he punched at an old, dried tree stump that was shaped
like a man and stood about five-and-a-half feet tall. Having pelted his own body with blows from head to foot,
he had ascertained that the most painful spots were the
solar plexus and the space between the eyebrows. He'd
also contemplated experimenting with the area that is tra-
ditionally said to be the most sensitive and vital spot on a
man's body, but eventually ruled out low blows as being
beneath a man of his dignity. He knew that the shins, too,
were quite vulnerable to pain, but kicking was the only
feasible means of attacking the shins, and Jirōbei shrank
from the thought of using his feet in a fight; such tactics

125

struck him as cowardly and underhanded. No, he would concentrate exclusively on the solar plexus and the space between the eyes. With a long knife he carved on the stump triangular marks that corresponded to these targets and punched away at them day after day. "Aren't you making a bit of a mistake? Or perhaps you're joking. You'd look awfully funny with the tip of your nose all purple and swollen. It would take a hundred days to return to normal. I do think you're making a mistake. . ." Then, suddenly, a shot between the eyes! A left to the solar plexus!

After a year of this training, the triangular marks on the stump were buried at the bottoms of two round depressions as deep as tea bowls. Jirōbei took stock. Now I can hit the spot every time, he told himself—a hundred shots, a hundred bull's-eyes. But that's no reason to relax. My opponent won't be standing still, like this stump. He'll be moving . . . It was then that Jirōbei's eye was caught by the waterwheels that stood at virtually every bend in the road. Dozens of full-bodied, limpid streams, fed by the snows melting on Mount Fuji, babbled past the foundations and under the verandas and through the gardens of Mishima's houses, and every night, on his way home from drinking, Jirōbei would subjugate one of the slow-turning, moss-covered waterwheels that harnessed these streams, whacking away, one by one, at the sixteen revolving blades. At first it was hard to find the range, and he didn't do much damage, but soon the sight of immobile waterwheels dangling their broken blades became common about the town.

Jirōbei bathed himself frequently in the cold waters of the streams. Sometimes he dived to the bottom and crouched there, motionless. He was taking into consideration the possibility of accidentally slipping and falling into the water during a fight. It could happen, what with streams crisscrossing the entire town. As an added precaution he tied his cotton bellyband an extra inch tighter to guard against letting excessive amounts of saké into his stomach, knowing that if he got too drunk, his legs might unexpectedly fail him.

Three years had passed. Thrice the festival at the Great Shrine had come and gone. The training was complete. Jirōbei looked more stolid and imposing than ever and was so muscle-bound that it took him a full minute just to turn his head to the left or right.

Relatives, being tied by blood, are quick to notice changes in one another. Ippei knew that Jirōbei was up to something. He had no idea exactly what sort of training his son was engaged in, but he sensed that he'd become a man to be reckoned with. Setting in motion the scheme he'd cherished for so long, he arranged for Jirōbei to be named his successor in the honorary post as head of the fire brigade. Jirōbei, by virtue of his unaccountably grave and commanding demeanor, immediately earned the trust and allegiance of the fire fighters; they called him "Chief" and treated him with the utmost respect, the sad upshot of which was that opportunities to challenge someone to a fight simply never presented themselves. Jirōbei was disconsolate to think that at this rate he might go to his grave without ever having partaken in a brawl. Each night his arms, bulging with the muscles he'd acquired through his rigorous training, itched maddeningly, and he scratched at them in a wretched frame of mind. Finally, out of sheer deviltry and desperation, and in hopes of creating an occasion to display his powers, he had his entire back tattooed.

The tattoo was of a blood-red rose some six inches across, around which were gathered five long, slender, mackerel-like fish that poked at the petals with pointed bills and were themselves encircled by a pattern of rippling blue wavelets that lapped at Jirōbei's ribs and spilled over onto his chest. So impressive was this tattoo that, far from exposing Jirōbei to the insults and provocative comments he was prepared for, it merely served to spread his fame up and down the Tōkaidō Road, and soon he was a hero not only to the firefighters but to all the ruffians and layabouts in town. Now his prospects for a fight were nil, and it was more than he could bear.

But then, just when he'd all but given up hope, a ray of light appeared. There was in Mishima at that time a wealthy saké brewer named Jinshūya Jōroku, the Shikamayas' greatest rival and competitor. Jōroku's saké was cloyingly sweet and darkish in color, and he himself was no exception to the rule that a brewer resembles his saké. A blackguard and an incorrigible womanizer, he was unsatisfied with the four mistresses he already had and was doing all he could think of to increase the number to five. It so happened that the arrow of his desire described an arc that passed over the Shikamaya home and pierced the grass-thatched roof of the calligraphy teacher's modest abode across the way. The calligraphy teacher didn't give in easily to Jōroku's demands concerning his daughter. Such was his despair on hearing them, in fact, that he twice attempted hara-kiri and would have succeeded had he not been discovered and restrained by members of his household. Jirōbei, having caught wind of this unjust state of affairs, awaited his chance, his muscles squirming and itching for action.

Three months later an opportunity arose. In early December, Mishima was visited by a rare heavy snowfall. Flurries began to fall at sunset, and soon enormous, peony-like flakes were floating down thick and fast. Some four inches of snow had accumulated on the ground when, all at once, the town's six warning bells began to sound. *Fire!* Jirōbei sauntered calmly outside. The house going up in flames was that of the tatami-mat maker who lived next door to Jōroku. Balls of fire danced and whirled over the roof of the poor fellow's house, and sparks billowed out like clouds of pinetree pollen, scattering far and wide; from time to time black smoke rose up like a tremendous, malevolent ghost, enveloping the entire roof; and the great flakes of snow, tinted with the bright colors of the flames, looked even more exquisite and precious as they fluttered down from the sky. When Jirōbei reached the scene, the firefighters were engaged in an argument with Jōroku. Jōroku wouldn't let them drench his house with water and demanded they knock down the tatami maker's roof to snuff the flames and keep them from spreading. The firefighters, for their part, maintained that to do so would be in violation of the firefighters' code.

"Jōroku-san," Jirōbei said, stepping forward. He kept his voice as low and restrained as possible and spoke with something almost like a smile on his lips. "Aren't you making a bit of a mistake? Or perhaps you're joking. You'd —"

"I say!" Jōroku interrupted him. "If it isn't the young master Shikamaya! I'm only joking, of course. Ha, ha! Just having a little fun with the boys, you know. Go right ahead, let the water flow!"

It didn't develop into a fight after all. There was nothing Jirōbei could do but stand there gazing dumbly at the fire.

Fight or no fight, however, the young chief once again saw his reputation grow as a result of this incident. For a long time afterwards the story was told among the firefighters of how fearsome, how like a very god, Jirōbei had looked facing down Jōroku that night, and how, as he stood in the glow of the fire, ten or more large snowflakes fell on his flushed, red cheeks and clung there without even melting.

On an auspicious day in February of the following year, Jirōbei finished construction of a new house on the outskirts of town. The ground floor consisted of three rooms that measured six, four-and-a-half, and three tatami mats in size, and upstairs in the rear was an eight-mat room with a spectacular view of Mount Fuji. On an even more auspicious day in March, he brought his new bride, the calligraphy teacher's daughter, to live with him. That night all the firefighters squeezed inside Jirōbei's new house to drink in celebration, and one by one as the night wore on they took turns entertaining the company with homespun party tricks and performances. It was morning before the last of them got up to deceive all the drunken and sleepy eyes with a magic trick involving a pair of saucers; when he was finished, a tiny splash of applause came from one corner, and with that the wedding banquet was brought to a close.

Jirōbei was vaguely aware that things had turned out pretty well for him after all, and he passed each day in a mild sort of stupefaction. His father, Ippei, was also heard to mutter, as he tapped out the ash of his long, slender pipe: "Well, that's one load off my mind." But then there occurred a tragic event that not even Ippei, with all his clearheaded wisdom, could have foreseen. One night during the second month after the wedding, Jirōbei was sitting at home with his wife, drinking the saké she poured for him, when he suddenly said: "I'm a hell of a fighter, you know. Here's what you do when you're fighting somebody: first you punch them between the eyes with a right, like this, then you slug 'em in the solar plexus with your left, like that." The demonstration was only in jest, of course, and he scarcely touched her, but his bride slumped to the floor, dead. Apparently those were, indeed, effective spots to hit a person. Jirōbei was arrested, charged with manslaughter, and sent to prison—punished for being all too skilled at his art.

Even in prison, that indomitable composure that one sensed about Jirōbei prevented him from being abused or looked down upon by the guards and earned him the respect of the other inmates, who lost no time in recognizing him as boss of the cellblock. Seated upon his throne of several mats stacked one atop the other, with the rest of the convicts gathered at his feet, Jirōbei would intone a mournful melody of his own invention, a melody that was not quite a song and not quite a chant:

> With cheeks flushed red,
> I whispered to the rocky crag:
> "I'm tough, you know!"
> The crag made no reply.

SABURŌ THE LIAR

nce upon a time, in the town of Fukaga-wa in old Edo, there lived a widower and scholar by the name of Haramiya Kōson, a specialist in Chinese religions. Kōson had one child, whose name was Saburō. People in the neighborhood were wont to remark that it was just like a scholar to be so perverse as to name his only son Saburō, which is of course a name normally reserved for third sons. The fact that no one could explain what it was that made that particular act so typical of schol-arly perversity was, it was said, precisely what made it so. Kōson was not very highly thought of in his neighborhood. Word had it that he was exceedingly stingy—so stingy, in fact, that according to a persistent rumor he habitually re-gurgitated half his rice to re-use as paste.

It was as a consequence of this miserliness of Kōson's that Saburō's lies first began to blossom. Until he was eight years old, Saburō never received a single sen of spending money, but was forced to pass his days memorizing say-ings of the ancient Chinese sages. Sniffling his perpetually runny nose and muttering the aphorisms to himself over and over, he would walk about the house working nails loose from the walls and pillars of all the rooms. As soon as he'd accumulated ten nails, he'd take them to a nearby junk dealer and sell them for one or two sen, which he'd invest in deep-fried dough cakes. Later on, when the junk dealer informed him that he could get about ten times as much money for books, Saburō began stealthily making off with one volume after another from his father's library. It was as he was stealing the sixth book that his father caught him. Tears streaming down his cheeks, Kōson chastised his wayward son with three quick blows to the head. Then he spoke. "To whip you at greater length would only cause both of us to work up an appetite in vain. I shall therefore leave your punishment at this. Sit down."

Saburō was forced to vow tearful repentance, and it was with this vow that his lies began.

That summer, he killed the next-door neighbor's pet dog. The dog was a Pekinese. One night it began to raise a horrible racket: long, drawn-out howls, frantic, scream-like yaps, exaggerated, moaning wails—a full repertoire of ghastly cries that made it sound as if it were suffering the agonies of the damned. When it had carried on without pause for an hour or so, Kōson spoke to his son, who was in the bed next to his, saying: "Go have a look." Saburō had been lying there with his head raised, blinking and listening. He got up, slid open the rain shutters, and looked outside. The Pekinese, tied to the neighbor's bamboo fence, was writhing on the ground. "Hold it down," said Saburō. In response, the Pekinese began to make a show of rolling in the dirt and chewing hungrily at the fence, as if it had gone quite mad, then proceeded to yap even more shrilly than before. Its infantile mentality inspired in Saburō a burning hatred. "Hold it down, hold it down," he muttered beneath his breath as he stepped into the garden, picked up a stone, and hurled it. The stone hit the Pekinese square in the head; it gave a short, piercing cry, spun its white, furry body about like a top, and dropped to the ground, dead. When Saburō had closed the rain shutters and got back in bed, his father asked in a sleepy voice what had happened. Saburō pulled the quilt up over his head and said: "It stopped barking. It appears to be ill. I shouldn't be surprised if it dies within a day or two."

During the autumn of that same year, Saburō killed a person. He pushed a playmate off the Kototoi Bridge into the Sumida River. He did it for no special reason; it was strictly on impulse—the sort of impulse that makes a man want to stick a pistol in his own ear and fire. The boy he pushed, the youngest son of a tofu peddler, moved his long, slender legs as he fell, taking three slow, waddling steps, as if trying to get a foothold on the air, then splashed through the surface of the water. When the current had carried the ring of ripples some yards downstream, a hand poked out from the center, clenched in a tight fist. Then it disappeared again. The ripples fell apart as they flowed along, and only when Saburō had watched the last of them vanish did he begin to wail at the top of his lungs. In response to his cries, people came running up and, looking at the spot Saburō pointed to as he sobbed, surmised what must have happened. One man who was particularly quick to jump to conclusions patted Saburō's shoulder and said: "You did well, calling for help. Your friend fell in, did he? Don't cry, we'll save him. You did well!" From the crowd three confident swimmers stepped forward, raced one another into the water, and proceeded to display their rather remarkable aquatic skills. All three of them, unfortunately, were more concerned with how they looked to the crowd than with actually searching for the tofu-peddler's son, as a result of which, when they finally did find him, he was already dead.

Saburō felt nothing, even when he and Kōson attended the boy's funeral together. It wasn't until he was ten or eleven that his secret crime began to torment him, and the anguish only resulted in bringing his lies into even fuller and more spectacular bloom. By lying to others, and to himself, he fervently tried to obliterate his crime from reality and from his own heart, and thus, in the course of growing up, he became a walking, talking mass of pre-varication.

By the time he reached the age of twenty, Saburō was, to all appearances, a meek and mild young man. When the Festival of the Dead came around, he sought and received the sympathy of people in his neighborhood by reminisc-ing, with many a melancholy sigh, about his late mother. This though Saburō's mother had died giving birth to him; he'd never known her and had never even spent any time thinking about her before.

As his skill at lying grew ever more remarkable, Saburō began to ghostwrite letters for two or three of the stu-dents who studied under Kōson. His specialty was writ-ing parents to ask for money. He would begin with a brief description of the weather and scenery, express an inno-cent hope that all was well with the beloved and respected parent, then delve right into the matter at hand. Nothing, to Saburō's mind, could be less effective than to begin with long, drawn-out passages full of groveling flattery and end with a plea for cash. The plea only made the flattery all the more transparent and gave the whole letter an air of sordid insincerity. Better to pluck up one's courage and get to the heart of the matter as quickly as possible. It was also advisable to keep things short and succinct. Like this:

We are about to begin our study of the Book of Songs. *If purchased from the local bookseller, the text costs twenty-two yen. Professor Kōson, however, having kindly taken into consideration the financial status of his students, has decided to order the books directly from China. The cost comes to fifteen yen, eighty sen per volume. Since passing up this opportunity would mean suffering a substantial loss, I should like to order one of the books from him as soon as possible. Please send fifteen yen, eighty sen posthaste . . .* After getting the request for money out of the way, one should then describe some trifling everyday occurrence. For example: *Yesterday, looking out my window, I watched a single hawk doing battle with any number of crows—truly a valiant, soul-stirring sight.* Or: *The day before yesterday, as I was taking a walk along the banks of the Sumida River, I found the most peculiar little flower. It had small petals, like those of a morning glory, or, rather, quite large petals, you might say, like a sweet pea, and was white, but on the reddish side—such a rare find that I dug it up, roots and all, and replanted it in a pot in my room . . .*

And so on, rambling leisurely along as if one had forgotten all about money, or anything else. The beloved father, reading this letter, would reflect upon the tranquility in his son's heart and, ashamed of the worldly cares that plagued his own, send off the cash with a smile. Saburō's letters really did have such an effect. More and more students flocked to him to ask that he write or dictate their correspondence, and when the money arrived they would invite him out on the town and spend every last sen. Before long, Kōson's little school began to prosper. Students from all over Edo, having heard of Saburō's tal-

ent, flocked there in hopes of picking up a few pointers
from the young master.

Being in such demand gave Saburō pause. To write or
dictate dozens of letters each day was too much trouble.
Why not publish? He could compile his methods for putting the touch on one's parents into a single volume and
have hundreds of copies printed up and sold at bookshops.
He soon saw the flaw in this plan, however: What if the
parents should buy and study the book themselves? He
could foresee the result easily enough—as could his students, whose fierce opposition helped convince him to
abandon the scheme. His desire to publish something had
now taken root, however, and finally he decided to pen a
novel about life in the pleasure quarters, such books being
all the rage in Edo at the time. Written in a mock-serious
tone, often opening with words like, "Ho, ho! I humbly
submit," and going on to describe all manner of nasty
pranks and underhanded deceptions, works of this sort
were the perfect medium for Saburō's talents. At the age of
twenty-two, he published two or three books in this genre
under the pen name of Professor Crapulus Blotto, and
they sold better than he'd ever dared dream they might.

One day, Saburō discovered his own masterpiece, a
volume entitled *In Lies Lies the Truth*, among the books
in his father's library, and casually asked him about it. "Is
Professor Blotto's novel any good?" Kōson made a sour
face before answering: "It most certainly isn't." Smiling,
Saburō told him the truth: "Professor Crapulus Blotto
is my *nom de plume*." Kōson, flustered but determined to
feign composure, noisily cleared his throat twice, then a
third time, and asked in a hoarse, conspiratorial whisper:
"How much did you make on it?"

Dazai Osamu

The masterpiece *In Lies Lies the Truth* was about the fascinating and comical life of a cynical young man named Master Misanthropos, who, when visiting the pleasure quarters, would pass himself off as an actor or a millionaire or a nobleman on a secret outing. So rich in versatility were Misanthropos's deceptions that the geisha and the male entertainers never doubted for a moment that he was who he said he was. His ruses were indistinguishable from reality, and in the end even Misanthropos himself ceased to doubt that it was all true—that he had become a millionaire overnight, or had awakened one morning to find himself an actor famous throughout the world. And so he passed a life of pleasure and gaiety, and it was only when he died that he reverted to being the impoverished Master Misanthropos. The novel was, one might say, based on Saburō's own life story. By the time he'd published it, his skill at lying was almost superhuman; whatever deception he chose to perpetrate was infused with a golden glow of truth. In the presence of Kōson he was a meek young man saturated with filial piety, to the students he was someone with unbelievable knowledge about the ways of the world, and at the pleasure quarters he was none other than the great actor Danjūrō or the lord of such-and-such a fief or the boss of the so-and-so gang, and in none of these roles was there the slightest hint of anything unnatural or fraudulent.

The following year, Kōson died. He left a will that said, in effect: "I'm a liar and a hypocrite. The further my heart strayed from the Great Learnings, the more I preached them. That I was able to live on in spite of this was due only to my love for my son, who never knew his dear mother. Knowing what a failure I was, I wanted somehow to make a success of this poor boy. Alas, it appears that he, too, is destined to fail. To this child of mine I leave my entire fortune—the fifty sen in change that I have accumulated over the past sixty years." Saburō read the will and paled. Then, with a sickly smile on his lips, he ripped it in two. He ripped the two pieces into four. Then he ripped those into eight. Kōson, who had spared his child the rod for fear of working up a costly appetite, who had been less concerned with his son's renown than with his royalties, and of whom it had been whispered throughout the neighborhood that he kept a jar full of gold buried beneath the house—this Kōson had passed quietly on, leaving a measly half a yen behind. This was the lie to end all lies. Saburō felt as if he could smell the unbearable stench of deception's final, sputtering fart.

He held his father's funeral at a nearby Nichiren Buddhist temple. Listening intently to the priest's frenzied beating of the drum, Saburō began to detect within its savage rhythm an uncontrollable fury and anxiety, along with a desperate sort of buffoonery that attempted to disguise those emotions. Surrounded by a dozen or more of Kōson's students, Saburō sat in his formal black kimono, fingering his prayer beads, staring at the edge of the tatami mat some three feet in front of him, and thinking. Lies are the silent farts that emanate from crime. His own lies had had as their starting point the murder he'd committed as a child. His father's lies had been squeezed out by the guilt that weighed upon him for the great crime of preaching a religion he no longer believed in. One lies to seek a bit of relief from a ponderous, suffocating reality, but the liar, like the drinker, gradually comes to need larger and larger doses. The lies become blacker and more complex, and they mesh and rub together until in the end they shine with the luster of truth. Saburō wasn't the only one for whom this

139

was the case, apparently. *In Lies Lies the Truth*. Suddenly remembering this title and feeling the words strike home as if for the first time, he smiled bitterly to himself. It was the very pinnacle of absurdity. Once he'd seen to the proper burial of Kōson's bones, Saburō resolved that from that day on he would lead a life free of lies. Everyone had a secret crime in his past. There was nothing to fear. No reason to feel inferior.

A life free of lies! Ah, but that, too, was, by definition, a lie. To praise good and condemn evil? Another lie. Surely a lie already dwelled in the heart of anyone who sought to make such distinctions and stand in judgment. Every way of life Saburō could think of seemed tainted, and he agonized over the problem night after sleepless night. Finally, however, he discovered an attitude that seemed to offer hope. He would learn to become an idiot, without will or emotion. To live like the wind. Saburō began to base all his daily actions on the astrological predictions in the almanac, and took pleasure only in the dreams he dreamed each night. Some were of fresh green fields in spring, others of lovely young maidens who set his heart to pounding.

Then, one morning as he was eating breakfast alone, a thought occurred to him. He shook his head and slapped his chopsticks down on the tray. He stood up and paced three times around the room, then folded his arms and stepped outside. He'd suddenly grown suspicious of his new pose. Pretending to be without will or emotion—was this not, in fact, the deepest recess of the liar's hell? How did making a conscious attempt to be an idiot qualify as a life free of lies? The greater his efforts, the thicker the layers of lies had become. To hell with it, then, he thought.

Romanesque

All that was left was the world of the unconscious. Though it was well before noon, Saburō set out for a drinking spot.

Parting the rope curtain and entering the place, he saw that, early in the day though it was, two customers were already there. And, wonder of wonders, who might they be but Tarō the Wizard and Jirōbei the Fighter? Tarō was seated at the southeast corner of the table, his smooth, plump cheeks flushed pink from the saké he drank as he twisted and twirled his long, dangling mustache. Jirōbei was encamped opposite him, in the northwest corner, and his swollen face gleamed with greasy sweat as he slowly swung his left arm in a wide, sweeping arc to take a drink, then held the cup up to eye level and gazed at it vacantly. Saburō took a seat halfway between them and started right in drinking. The three had never met before, of course. They sized one another up, each of them stealing furtive glances—Tarō with his narrow eyes half closed, Jirōbei taking a full minute to turn his head to either side, and Saburō with the restless, darting gaze of a hunted animal. Little by little, as the saké gradually did its work, the three of them edged closer together. When their intoxication, which each had struggled to contain, finally erupted, Saburō was the first to speak.

"It seems to me that the fact that we happen to be drinking together like this, at this time of day, means that there's some sort of bond between us. Especially when you consider where we are: Edo teems with so many people that it's said if you walk half a block you're in a different world, yet here we are in the same little shop at the same time of the same day—it's like a miracle."

141

Tarō gave a great yawn. "I drink because I like saké. Quit looking at me like that," he drawled, and raised his neckerchief to mask the lower half of his face.

Jirōbei spoke up after slapping the table and leaving a depression four inches long and an inch deep. "You're right," he said. "You could call it a bond. I just got out of prison."

Saburō asked what he'd been in for.

"Well, here's what happened . . ." In a barely fathomable murmur, Jirōbei proceeded to tell his entire life story. When he finished, a single tear rolled down his cheek and dropped into his saké cup, which he then drained at a gulp.

Saburō pondered the tale for a while and finally said, by way of preamble, that he felt as if they were brothers, then launched into his own story, pausing after every sentence in an effort to prevent so much as a single lie from escaping his lips.

Jirōbei, after listening for some time, declared, "I don't know what the hell you're talking about," and promptly fell asleep in his chair. But Tarō, who had until then done nothing but yawn in boredom, now opened his narrow eyes as wide as they would go and listened intently.

When the story was finished, Tarō languidly removed his neckerchief mask. "You said your name was Saburō? Listen, I understand exactly how you feel. My name's Tarō. I'm from Tsugaru. I came to Edo two years ago, and I've been loafing about in places like this ever since. You want to hear my story?"

In his usual sleepy tone of voice, Tarō related his own experiences, down to the smallest detail. No sooner had he finished than Saburō gave a great shout: "I know! I know just what you mean!"

The shout awoke Jirōbei. Opening his cloudy eyes, he turned to Saburō. "What's all the racket about?" he said.

Saburō was ashamed of his own raptures. Ecstasy is the ultimate lie. He tried to force himself to be calm, but his intoxication wouldn't permit it. His half-hearted attempt to control himself only provoked the rebelliousness in his soul, and at last he threw all caution to the wind and spat out a lie of enormous proportions. "We three are artists!" he proclaimed, but all it did was further fuel the fire of prevarication. "We're brothers, we three! Now that we've met, not even death can separate us. Our day will come, and soon—I'm certain of it! Listen, I'm a writer. I'm going to write the stories of Tarō the Wizard and Jirōbei the Fighter and, with your leave, my own story as well, to offer the world three models for living. Who cares what people say?" Now the flames of Saburō the Liar's lies were burning at maximum intensity. "We're artists, I tell you! We needn't bow down to anyone, though he be the noblest and richest prince in the land. For men like us, money carries no more weight than a falling leaf!"

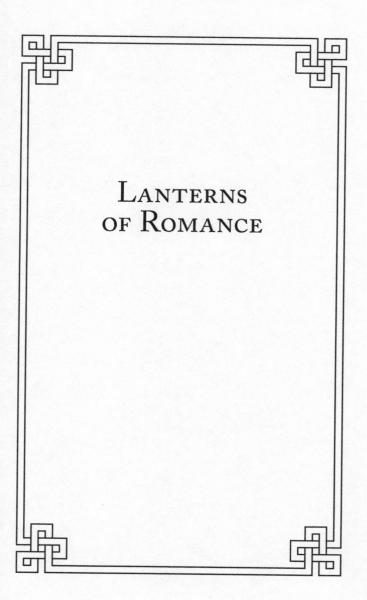

LANTERNS
OF ROMANCE

The members of the family of the famous painter Irie Shinnosuke, who passed away some eight years ago, all seem a bit on the eccentric side. This is not to say that the family is abnormal; it's possible that their way of life is as it should be and that the rest of us are the abnormal ones, but, in any case, the atmosphere of the Irie home is decidedly different from most. It was this atmosphere that suggested to me the idea for "On Love and Beauty," a short story I wrote some time ago.

The story opened with descriptions of the five Irie sons and daughters and went on to sketch a certain insignificant little incident. It was a naive, sentimental, and trivial work, to be sure, but one that I nonetheless remain quite fond of, although I must admit that my affection is not so much for the story itself as for the family described therein. I loved that family. I cannot pretend that my depiction of their household conforms precisely to the facts, however. To put it in such overblown terms causes me more than a little embarrassment, but my account included certain elements that fell short of Goethe's ideals of "poetry and truth." There are even a few colossal lies mixed in. Most regrettable of all is that, although I wrote about the five brothers and sisters and their kind and sagacious mother, the structure of the story was such that I was forced to take the liberty of omitting the grandmother and grandfather. This, I now realize, was an unwarrantable measure. It would appear that, in the final analysis, one simply can't give a complete picture of the Irie household without including this venerable couple, and I'd like to say a few words about them now.

First, however, I must make one further disclaimer. What I am about to describe is not the Irie household as it exists today, but as it was four years ago, when I began to scribble the previous story. Things have changed for the family since that time. Marriage, and even death, have intervened. Compared to four years ago, the atmosphere of the household is somewhat gloomier. And it is no longer possible for me to drop by the house for a casual visit, as I once used to do. The five brothers and sisters, and I myself, have gradually grown more adult, more polite, more guarded—have become, in short, "members of society"—and when we do on occasion meet, it's not the least bit fun. To speak plainly, I no longer have much interest in the Irie family. If I am to write about them, I want to write about them as they were in the past. Having made that much clear . . .

The grandfather, at that time, spent each day at his leisure. If it is true that an uncommon romanticism flowed through the veins of the Irie family, it most likely originated with this elderly gentleman. In the prime of his life he had managed a rather successful trading operation in Yokohama, but far from opposing the decision of Shinnosuke, his late son and only heir, to enter the Art Academy rather than study business, the old man actually boasted about it to those around him. That's the sort of man the grandfather was. Even now that he was advanced in years and retired from business, he refused to confine himself to sitting around the Irie house in Kōjimachi. He was past eighty, and yet after dressing immaculately each morning as if he had some important affair to attend to, he would make his escape the moment no one was watching, slipping out though the back gate with astonishing speed. After walking at a brisk pace for two or three blocks, he would glance back to make sure he wasn't being followed, then pull a hunting cap from his pocket. The cap was a gaudy checkered specimen that he'd worn lovingly for forty years. It had always been an eyesore, and was now crumpled with age, but without it a walk simply wasn't a walk.

With this cap set jauntily on the back of his head, then, he would set out for the Ginza. There he'd enter Shiseidō and order hot chocolate, a single cup of which he'd sit over and sip at for as long as an hour or two. He'd survey the entire room, and if he happened to see one of his old business acquaintances with a young geisha or some other companion of that sort, he would immediately call the man over in a loud voice, insist that the couple join him in his booth, and proceed to hold them captive as he drawled out a series of caustic remarks. He derived unspeakable pleasure from this.

On the way home from these excursions, the grandfather would often buy a meager gift for someone in the family. He was, apparently, plagued by a certain sense of guilt over his unorthodox behavior, and recently he'd been making a concerted effort to get on the good side of everyone else in the house. To this end he'd come up with the idea of conferring a medal of honor upon the family member who performed the most meritorious service each week. The medal was one he'd devised himself by passing a red silk cord through a hole punched in a silver Mexican coin. Unfortunately, no one wanted this prize very badly. It was a matter of consternation to all of them that the person who received the medal was obliged to wear it, whenever at home, for the entire week.

The mother, being a model of filial piety toward her father-in-law, would express gratitude whenever she received the award and promptly attach it to her sash, albeit in as inconspicuous a location as possible. Each time she allotted the grandfather an extra bottle of beer for his nightcap she was awarded the medal then and there, like it or not. When the eldest son blundered, on occasion, into having the medal bestowed upon him for such services as accompanying the grandfather to a music hall, he accepted his fate with the good grace one would expect of a man of his staid and serious nature, and would wear it prominently around his neck for the entire week. The elder daughter and second son avoided being put into that position. The elder daughter's clever ruse was to proclaim herself quite unworthy of the honor and positively decline to accept. The second son, for his part, had gone so far as to stuff the medal in his dresser drawer and claim to have lost it, although the grandfather had seen through this bit of subterfuge at once and sent the younger daughter to search his room. She was unfortunate enough to find the prize, as a result of which she was designated the next recipient. The grandfather was clearly partial to the younger daughter. Though she was the most self-centered member of the family and devoid of any special merit whatsoever, he was forever looking for an excuse to confer his award upon her. When this happened, she generally put the medal away in her purse and left it there the entire week. She alone was permitted such exceptional behavior.

The youngest son was the only one who had the slightest desire to be awarded the prize. Even he felt somehow awkward and embarrassed when obliged to wear it around his neck, yet he always experienced a certain sense of loss the moment it was taken away from him and given to someone else; and occasionally, when the younger daughter was out, he would sneak into her room, open her purse, and gaze nostalgically at the medal inside. The grandmother had never once been awarded the medal, for the simple reason that from the very beginning she had emphatically refused to have anything to do with it. Being a plain-spoken woman, she had described the entire idea as "imbecilic."

It would be difficult to give a clear picture of the grandmother without touching upon her affection for the youngest son, who was quite simply the apple of her eye. He once took up the study of hypnotism and attempted, without the least success, to mesmerize his grandfather, mother, and brothers and sisters. One by one they returned his gaze, peering at him curiously as he tried to put them to sleep. Everyone enjoyed a good laugh over this except the youngest son himself, who was on the verge of tears and sweating profusely by the time he turned to his last subject, the grandmother. She fell into a deep sleep almost immediately, nodding in her chair, and innocently answered the hypnotist's solemn questions.

"Grandmother, you can see a flower, can't you?"

"Yes. It's very pretty."

"What sort of flower is it?"

"It's a lotus."

"Grandmother, what do you love most?"

"You."

This reply gave the hypnotist pause.

"Who is 'you'?"

"Why, it's you. Kazuo [the youngest son]."

The rest of the family burst into laughter, which snapped the grandmother out of her trance, but the hypnotist had at least managed to save face. Later, however, when the ever-serious eldest son worriedly asked the grandmother if she'd really been in a trance, she chuckled and muttered: "What do *you* think?"

I could go on and on about the Irie family, but for now I'd prefer to present you with a rather long story constructed by the family members themselves. As anyone familiar with them knows, the Irie brothers and sisters all have a certain fondness for the literary arts, and from time to time they gather to tell a story by turns. This often takes place, at the urging of the eldest son, when they've assembled in the drawing room on a cloudy Sunday and find that boredom has begun to weigh upon them. The game begins with one of them describing whatever sort of character might pop into his or her mind, and the others take turns concocting that character's destiny. Simpler tales they do on an impromptu basis, each delivering his or her portion orally, but when the story offers interesting possibilities they take the precaution of writing their episodes out and passing the manuscript around. They presumably have a number of these co-authored narratives stashed away somewhere. Occasionally the grandfather, grandmother, and mother help out, and this appears to have been the case with the rather long story we're concerned with today.

— II —

The youngest son, though not very accomplished at this sort of endeavor, was generally the one who started off, and he generally made a mess of things. But this time he really intended to put his heart into it. When, with the five days of New Year's vacation before them, the brothers and sisters grew bored and decided to engage in the usual storytelling pastime, the youngest son once again expressed a desire to take the lead. "Let me start," he said. "I'll go first." It was always the same, and as usual his elder brothers and sisters just smiled ruefully and let him have his way. This being the first story of the year, they decided to take special care and write it out by turns. The deadline for each contributor was to be the morning of the day after receiving the manuscript. Each therefore had one entire day to conceive and write his or her portion, and the story would be complete by the fifth night or the sixth morning. During these five days, all of the brothers and sisters would be slightly on edge and aware of having a certain rare sense of purpose in their lives.

The youngest son, then, had once again expressed a desire to go first, and since his wish had been granted he was to begin the story, but unfortunately he had no idea what to write. He appeared to be suffering a block. He wished he hadn't volunteered to start. On New Year's Day, the other brothers and sisters all went out to enjoy themselves, and the grandfather too had disappeared early in the morning, decked out in tails. The only ones left in the house were the mother, the grandmother, and the youngest son, who sat in his room sharpening and resharpening a pencil. After some hours had gone by, he could feel tears welling up, and at last, utterly desperate, he aban-

153

doned himself to a sinister plot. Plagiarism. He felt he had no choice. His heart pounding, he leafed through various books from his shelf—a copy of *Grimm's Fairy Tales*, a volume of stories by Hans Christian Andersen, *The Adventures of Sherlock Holmes*, and so on. Stealing a little bit from here, a little bit from there, he somehow managed to throw something together.

Once upon a time, in the middle of a forest in the north country, there lived a horrible, ugly old witch. Though a truly vile old hag in every way, she was kind to one person—her only daughter, Rapunzel. The witch was absolutely devoted to Rapunzel, and every day she combed out her hair with a golden comb. Rapunzel was a beautiful girl. She was also a spirited, sassy child, and by the time she turned fourteen she had ceased to listen to anyone. There were times, in fact, when she went so far as to scold her own mother. But the witch so doted on her daughter that she would merely smile and beg forgiveness.

It was the time of year when cold north winds blow through the forest, leaving the trees more scantily clad with each passing day, and preparations for winter had begun at the witch's house. One evening a wonderful prize wandered into the enchanted forest. A handsome young prince, mounted on horseback, had lost his way in the gathering darkness. He was the sixteen-year-old son of the king of this land. Engrossed in the chase during a hunting expedition, he'd lost contact with his servants and was unable to find the path back home. With his golden armor shining like a torch in the dim light, there was small chance that the witch would fail to notice him. She flew out of her house with the speed of the wind and in no time at all had pulled the prince down from his saddle.

"How nice and plump this boy is!" she gurgled. "Just look at that tender white flesh . . . Fattened on walnuts, no doubt." The old witch had long, sparse whiskers, and eyebrows that hung down over her eyes. "He's like a fat little lamb! I wonder how he tastes. Pickled in brine, he ought to be just the thing for the long winter nights!"

Grinning with delight, she unsheathed her dagger and had laid its edge on the prince's white throat when, suddenly, she let out a cry of pain. She'd just been bitten on the left ear by her own daughter, who'd jumped on her back and refused to let go.

The old witch, who loved and pampered Rapunzel so, did not lose her temper but forced a smile and cried: "Rapunzel! Forgive me!"

Rapunzel shook her by the shoulders. "I want to play with this pretty boy," she whined. "Give him to me." Having grown up spoiled and selfish, she was an obstinate child, and once she'd made a demand she never gave in. Knowing this, the old witch agreed to put off killing and salting the prince for just one night.

"Very well, very well, you can have him. He'll be your guest tonight, and we'll treat him to a splendid feast. But you must give him back to me tomorrow. All right, dear?"

Rapunzel nodded.

That night, the prince was shown the utmost in witch hospitality but was nonetheless frightened out of his wits, not knowing if he was to live or die. Dinner consisted of frogs grilled on skewers; the skin of a pit viper stuffed with the fingers of little children; a salad of death cups, wet mouse noses, and the innards of green caterpillars; swamp-scum liqueur; and a nitric acid wine, fresh from the grave it was brewed in. This was all topped off with a confection of rusty nails and fragments of church-window glass. The prince felt sick just looking at it all and didn't touch a thing, but the old witch and Rapunzel gobbled and guzzled and raved about how delicious it all was. Every dish was a delicacy they'd set aside for a special occasion.

After dinner Rapunzel took the prince by the hand and led him to her room. They were about the same height, and once they were inside she put her arm around his shoulder, peered into his eyes, and whispered: "As long as you don't come to hate me, I won't let anyone kill you. You're a prince, right?"

Thanks to the witch's daily combing, Rapunzel's hair glistened as if it were made of threads spun from the purest gold, and it hung down almost to her knees. Her angelic, round face made one think of a wild yellow rose, her lips were small and as red as strawberries, and her eyes were dark and clear, with a hint of melancholy deep inside them. The prince thought he'd never seen such a beautiful girl before.

"Yes," he answered quietly. Some of the tension inside him melted away with the reply, and tears began to run down his cheeks.

Rapunzel peered at him with those clear, dark eyes and nodded. "Even if you come to hate me, I won't let anyone kill you. If you come to hate me, see, I'll have to kill you myself." She, too, had begun to weep, but suddenly burst out laughing and wiped her tears with the back of her hand. Then she wiped the prince's tears as well. "Come on," she said brightly. "Tonight you'll sleep with me, where I keep all my pets." And with that she led him to her bedroom. On the floor were blankets and a pile of straw. The prince looked up at the ceiling to see perhaps a hundred pigeons, all resting on perches and rafters. They appeared to be asleep but stirred slightly when he and Rapunzel approached.

"All these are mine," Rapunzel said. She snatched up the pigeon nearest her, held it by the feet, and shook it. The startled pigeon flapped its wings frantically, and Rapunzel thrust it in the prince's face and cried: "Kiss it!" Then she nodded toward a large bamboo cage in one corner of the room and said: "See those crows over there? They're the gangsters of the forest. There are ten of them, but they're bad boys, so I've got to keep them locked up or they'll fly away. And over here is my old sweetheart, Bae." She went to the opposite corner of the room and came back pulling a deer along by its antlers. The deer had a shiny copper ring around its neck, attached to a thick iron chain. "This one, too, if I don't keep him chained down, he'll try to run away. Why don't they want to stay with me? Oh, well, it doesn't matter. Every night I take a knife and tickle Bae's throat with it. He gets really scared when I do that, and starts wriggling around like anything." Rapunzel pulled a long, shiny knife from a crack in the wall and began stroking the deer's neck with the blade. The poor deer squirmed in distress and broke out in a greasy sweat. Rapunzel laughed.

"Do you keep that knife next to you when you sleep too?" the prince asked warily.

"Sure," said Rapunzel. "I always go to sleep hugging my knife. You never know what might happen. But never mind that. It doesn't matter. Let's go to bed. I want you to tell me how you ended up wandering into this forest."

The two of them lay down side by side on the straw, and the prince haltingly explained how he'd got lost and separated from his servants.

"Do you miss them?" she asked him.

"Yes."

"You want to go back to your castle?"

"Yes. Yes, I do."

"I hate children who pout!" Rapunzel said, sitting up suddenly. "It's better to look happy. I have two loaves of bread and some ham. You can eat that if you get hungry on the way home . . . Well? What are you waiting for?"

The prince jumped to his feet, overjoyed, but Rapunzel remained calm and composed. There was something almost maternal about her now.

"Oh, and put on these fur boots. You can have them. It'll be cold out there. I don't want you to get cold. And these are my mother's fingerless gloves. Shove your hands in. See? Now they look just like my ugly old mother's hands!"

As tears of gratitude rolled down the prince's face, Rapunzel dragged the deer out of its corner and unchained it.

"Bae. I'm going to miss tickling you with my knife, because you look so funny when I do, but never mind that. I'm going to set you free now. Take this boy back to the castle. He says he wants to go back. It doesn't matter. You're the only one who can run faster than the old woman. I want you to run as hard as you can."

The prince climbed on the deer's back.

"Thank you, Rapunzel. I'll never forget you."

"None of that matters. Run, Bae! Don't let our guest fall off, or you'll be sorry!"

"Goodbye," said the prince.

"Yeah, yeah. Goodbye," Rapunzel said, and burst into tears.

The deer flew through the darkness like an arrow. Leaping over thickets, it wound its way out of the forest, crossed a lake in a single bound, and in no time at all left behind a wilderness of howling wolves and screeching crows, cutting through the air with a rocketlike whistling sound.

"You mustn't look back," the deer said as it ran. "The old witch is chasing us. But don't worry. The only thing faster than me is a shooting star. You mustn't forget Rapunzel's kindness, though. She's a willful girl, but she's very lonely. Well, here we are."

Scarcely before he'd realized what was happening, the prince found himself standing in front of the castle. He felt as if he were dreaming.

Ah, but poor Rapunzel! This time the old witch was furious with her for letting such a valuable catch escape. She said Rapunzel's selfishness had gone too far this time, and locked her up in a dark tower deep in the forest. The tower had neither a door nor stairs, only one small window in a little room at the top. This was where Rapunzel was to spend her days and nights from then on. Poor, poor Rapunzel! A year passed, another year passed, and still she sat in the dark little room where, unbeknownst to anyone, she grew ever more beautiful. In her solitude she'd become a pensive young woman, and never for a single moment did she forget about her prince. Sometimes, overcome with loneliness, she sang for the moon and stars. The sorrow in her voice made the birds and trees in the forest weep, and even the moon would grow misty listening to her. Once a month the old witch would come to check on the girl, and to leave clean clothing and food, for she still loved her daughter and couldn't bear to see her starve. But only she, with her invisible wings, was able to enter or leave through the tower window.

Three years, four years passed, and now Rapunzel was eighteen years old. Alone in the dark room, not even she was aware of her shining beauty, or of her own flowerlike fragrance.

In the autumn of that year, the prince went out hunting again and once again lost his way in the forest. As he was wandering helplessly about, trying to find the path back home, a sorrowful song reached his ears. The voice touched his heart and moved him powerfully, and he staggered toward it until finally he came to the base of the tower. Perhaps, he thought, it was Rapunzel. The prince, too, you see, had never forgotten the beautiful girl he'd met four years before.

"Show me your face!" he shouted. "Please don't sing such a sorrowful song."

Rapunzel peeked out from the small window atop the tower. "Who are you, to say that to me? Sorrowful songs are the salvation of sorrow-filled hearts. You just don't understand the sadness of others."

"Ah! Rapunzel!" The prince was beside himself with joy. "Don't you remember me?"

Rapunzel's cheeks went pale for a moment, then flushed with a faint, rosy glow. She had not yet lost all the pig-headedness of her younger days, however.

"Rapunzel? She died four years ago!" she said in the coldest tone of voice she could manage. Then she drew a deep breath, intending to burst into hearty laughter, but all that came out was a choking sob. It was then that the birds of the forest began to sing, all at once, a peculiar song:

> *That child's hair is a bridge of gold!*
> *That child's hair is a rainbow bridge!*

Their voices reached Rapunzel's ears even as she wept, and she was suddenly struck by a wonderful flash of inspiration. She wound her long, lovely hair twice, three times around her left hand and took up a pair of scissors in her right. By now her shiny locks hung all the way to the floor, yet without the least hesitation or regret she clipped them off, then wove the strands

161

together into a single long rope—the most beautiful rope under the sun. And then, after securing one end to the window ledge, she climbed out and slid down that exquisite golden cable to the ground.

"Rapunzel!" The prince gazed at her, enraptured, but Rapunzel, for her part, had no sooner reached the ground than she was overcome with shyness. She could not even bring herself to speak, and it was all she could do to place her own fair hand on top of the prince's.

"Now, Rapunzel, it's my turn to help *you*. No, not just now—let me help you for the rest of my life." The prince was twenty now, a solid, upstanding young man. Rapunzel smiled at him faintly and nodded.

The two of them left the forest and ran as fast as they could, hoping to cross the wilderness before the old witch could find them out. Fortunately, they made it back safe and sound to the castle, where they were greeted with cheers.

It was only with great effort that the youngest son had managed to write this far, and now his mood turned sour. It was a failure. This wouldn't serve as the beginning of a story at all—he'd written all the way to the ending. His elder brothers and sisters were sure to laugh at him once again. He racked his brains. It was already growing dark, and all the others seemed to have returned from their outings; he could hear their cheerful, laughing voices down in the drawing room, and suffered an indescribable sense of solitude. Then a savior arrived, in the form of his grandmother. She'd been beside herself with concern for the poor youngest son, holed up alone in his room.

"At it again, are you?" she said as she entered the room. "Did you write something good?"

"Go away!" He was in a nasty mood.

"You've blundered again, haven't you? You shouldn't enter this silly sort of competition—you know it's not your forte. Let me see."

"You wouldn't understand!"

"No need to get hysterical. Let me see." She took her spectacles from her sash and read the youngest son's fairy tale aloud in a soft voice. "My, my," she said, chuckling. "Who'd have expected something like this from a child your age? It's interesting. You've done an excellent job. But there's no way to continue it."

"I know that."

"That's the problem, isn't it? If I were you, this is what I'd write: 'The two of them were greeted at the castle with cheers. But unhappiness lay ahead for them.' What do you think of that? A prince and the daughter of a witch—it's just too great a social gap. Regardless of how much they love each other, there's sure to be trouble. This sort of pairing is bound to bring unhappiness. See what I mean?" She poked the youngest son in the shoulder with her forefinger.

"I know that. I know that much. Go away! I've got my own ideas."

"Oh, is that so?" the grandmother said calmly. She knew more or less what his "own ideas" would amount to. "Hurry up and write it, then, and come on down to the drawing room. You must be hungry. You can have some rice cake and play a game of cards with the others. This writing competition is silly. Leave the rest to your big sister. She's very good at this, you know."

Once he'd chased his grandmother out, the youngest son picked up his pen again and added a few more lines.

But unhappiness lay ahead. There's just too great a social gap between a prince and the daughter of a witch. Misfortune was about to befall them. I'll leave it to my elder sister to explain. Please take good care of Rapunzel.

Thus he wrote—exactly as his grandmother had suggested—and breathed a sigh of relief.

— III —

It was the second day of the new year. Immediately after eating her rice cake with the rest of the family, the elder daughter retired alone to her study. She was wearing a white woolen sweater with a small artificial yellow rose pinned to the breast. Sitting on a cushion before her little writing desk, her legs tucked up beside her, she took off her glasses and smiled to herself as she vigorously polished the lenses with a handkerchief. Putting the glasses back on, she blinked exaggeratedly before adopting, suddenly, a solemn expression. She resettled on the cushion, sitting rigidly on her knees, and sank into contemplation. It was some minutes before she picked up her fountain pen and began to write.

The real story always begins where the love story ends. In most films, the word *Finis* is flashed on the screen the moment the happy couple are joined together, but what we, the audience, want to know, is what sort of life begins for them at that point. Life is by no means a drama consisting of one thrilling moment after another. We are born to spend most of our days in the midst of bland, bleak reality. Our prince and Rapunzel, who, though still mere children, had experienced a powerful bond of affection during the brief moment they were thrown together, discovered during their separation that they were unable to forget each other for a single instant, and after years of tribulation they succeeded in reuniting as adults. But that is far from being where the story ends. What remains to be told, what needs to be told, is the story of their life together from that point on. Though the prince and Rapunzel had escaped hand in hand from the enchanted forest,

165

crossed the vast wilds in a night and a day, forgoing food and drink and conversation, and finally succeeded in reaching the castle, a hard road still lay ahead of them.

Both Rapunzel and the prince were exhausted when they arrived at the castle, but at first there was no time to rest. The king, the queen, and all the servants were overjoyed to see the prince safe and sound, and they bombarded him with questions about his latest ordeal. When it became obvious that the extraordinary beauty standing modestly behind him with her head bowed was none other than the girl who'd saved his life four years earlier, their joy only doubled.

Rapunzel was treated to a perfumed bath, dressed in a lovely sheer gown, then shown to a bed with a mattress so thick and soft as to conform to every curve of her body, where she fell into such a deep sleep that she scarcely even seemed to be breathing. She slept a very long time, and when she'd finally had all the rest her body needed and awoke wide-eyed, like a ripe, juicy fig falling to the ground with a plop, she found the prince standing beside her pillow in full regalia, his vitality thoroughly restored.

Rapunzel was frantic with shame and embarrassment. She sat up and said: "I'm going home. Where's my dress?"

"Silly girl," said the prince complacently. "You're wearing it."

"I mean the dress I wore in the tower. Give it back. My mother sewed that dress for me out of the finest cloth, cloth she gathered from every corner of the earth."

"Silly girl," the prince said again in the same carefree tone of voice. "Do you miss her already?"

Rapunzel nodded. And then emotion welled up inside her, and she began to weep. It wasn't that she couldn't face being without her mother in a castle full of strangers—she'd resigned herself to that before fleeing. Nor could anyone say that the old woman had been a good mother to her; although even if she had been, it wouldn't have mattered. The nature of any young woman is such that as long as she's with the one she loves, her birth family is only a secondary concern. Rapunzel wasn't weeping out of loneliness, but out of shame and frustration. Having fled blindly to the castle, she'd been dressed in that exquisite sheer gown and shown to that soft, downy bed, where she'd fallen asleep, dead to the world; then, on awaking and seeing the situation with clear eyes, she'd been struck by the realization that she, the daughter of a despicable witch, was out of her element, a realization that made her feel demeaned and humiliated. Was this not why she'd blurted out that she was going home? It seems that she did indeed still retain some of the recalcitrance and willfulness she'd evinced as a child. The prince, for his part, having never known real hardship, was not likely to understand these feelings of hers. He was bewildered by Rapunzel's sudden tears.

"You're still tired," he decided offhandedly. "And you're hungry. We'll have them prepare breakfast." And with that he breezed out of the room.

Five ladies-in-waiting came for Rapunzel and gave her another perfumed bath, then dressed her in a crimson gown of thick velvet. They powdered her face and hands lightly, skillfully bound up her cropped golden hair, and secured a string of pearls around her neck. When at last Rapunzel rose serenely to her feet, the five let out a simultaneous sigh of admiration. Never before had any of them seen—nor could they imagine ever seeing again—such an elegant and stunning young lady.

Rapunzel was shown to the dining room. The king, queen, and prince stood by the table, waiting for her with radiant smiles.

"You look lovely," the king said, spreading his arms wide to welcome her.

"Doesn't she, though?" The queen nodded contentedly. Neither she nor her husband was the least bit arrogant or pretentious; both were gentle and compassionate people.

Rapunzel smiled somewhat sadly as she returned their greetings.

"Have a seat." The prince took Rapunzel's hand and led her to the table. "You can sit here," he said, "right next to me." The expression on his face was so triumphant as to be almost comical.

The king and queen took their seats, smiling their gentle smiles, and soon they all began to enjoy a congenial meal—all, that is, except Rapunzel, who was quite at a loss. She had no idea how to go about eating the succession of dishes that were served. Even when, by stealing glances at the prince beside her and imitating what he did, she managed to get the food to her mouth, the strange taste of the royal delicacies only nauseated the girl who'd grown up eating her mother's salads of caterpillar innards and maggots boiled in soy sauce. She did think the egg dish quite good, although the eggs of chickens struck her as no match for those of the forest crows.

There was no lack of topics for conversation at the table. The prince told about his terrifying experience of four years before and boasted of his most recent adventure, and the king, deeply impressed with each incident his son recounted, nodded emphatically and drank toast after toast, the upshot of which was that before long her was so thoroughly drunk that his wife had to carry him piggy-back out of the room.

As soon as Rapunzel was alone with the prince, she spoke to him in a quiet voice.

"I'd like to step outside. I don't feel very well."

She was deathly pale, but the prince was in such high spirits that it didn't even occur to him to be concerned. It seems that when people are in a state of euphoria, they don't always notice the suffering of others. Rapunzel's wan complexion didn't worry him in the least. He stood up and light-heartedly said: "You ate too much. All you need is a walk in the garden."

It was a lovely day outside. Though summer was long past, a variety of flowering plants were in bloom in the castle garden. At last Rapunzel smiled.

"I feel much better now. It's so dark inside the castle, I thought it was nighttime."

169

"Nighttime? You were fast asleep from yesterday afternoon until this morning. You slept so deeply you hardly seemed to be breathing. For a moment I thought you were dead!"

"It would be fine if the girl from the forest had died and awakened to find herself transformed into a lady of quality . . . but when I woke up I was still the witch's daughter." Rapunzel said this with genuine sorrow, but the prince took it as a joke and laughed heartily.

"You don't say. Ha ha! You poor thing!"

When they came to a spot in the shadow of a hedge of thorny shrubs where small, pure white, and very fragrant flowers were blooming in profusion, the prince stopped suddenly, and the look in his eyes grew serious. He took Rapunzel in his arms and squeezed her as if trying to crush every bone in her body, and then, without further warning, he began to do something that seemed like the act of a madman. Rapunzel bore up patiently. It wasn't the first time this had happened. He'd done the same sort of thing three times during the sleepless night and day they'd fled the forest and crossed the wilderness.

"You'll never leave me now, will you?" the prince said softly, once his passion had subsided and he and Rapunzel were strolling along again side by side. They stepped out from behind the thorny shrubs and headed toward a little pond where water lilies bloomed. His question struck Rapunzel as a queer one, and she laughed.

"What? What happened?" The prince peered at her face. "What's so funny?"

"I'm sorry. It's just that you act so serious, I can't help laughing. Where could I possibly go? I waited four years in that tower for you." When they reached the edge of the pond, Rapunzel felt tears welling up; she collapsed to the green grass and sat there looking up at the prince. "Did the king and queen give us their blessing?"

"Of course." The prince put on his carefree look once again and sat down next to her. "After all, I owe my life to you."

Rapunzel buried her face in his lap and unleashed a torrent of tears.

A few days later an extravagant and lavish wedding party was held at the castle. That night the trembling bride looked like an angel who'd lost her wings. And as a month, then two months went by, the prince only fell all the more deeply in love with this exotic, wild rose whose upbringing had been so different from his own. He grew ever more fascinated with her outlandish thoughts, her almost savagely spirited manner, her fearlessness and courage, and her naive, childlike questions.

The cold winter had passed. It was growing warmer by the day, and the first flowers of spring had begun to open their petals. Rapunzel and the prince were strolling side by side in the garden once again. Rapunzel was with child.

"It's strange . . . It's really so strange . . ."

"Here we go again. Another one of your questions, right?" The prince was twenty-one now and seemed a good deal more mature and sure of himself. "What

171

sort of question is it this time, I wonder. The one the other day was a real gem: 'Where is God?'"

Rapunzel bowed her head slightly and giggled. Then she looked up and said:

"Am I a woman?"

The prince was taken aback by this question, but chose to reply in a rather pompous tone.

"Well, you're most certainly not a man."

"So I'll have a baby, and I'll become an old woman?"

"You'll be a beautiful old woman."

"I won't." There was a smile on Rapunzel's face, but it was a very sad smile. "I won't have a baby."

"Now why would you say something like that?" The prince's tone was one of easy confidence, as if he were indulging a child.

"I didn't sleep last night, thinking about it. If I give birth, it will turn me suddenly into an old woman. You'll love and cherish only the baby, and I'll just be in the way. Nobody will care about me anymore. I know. I'm a stupid girl of lowly birth, and once I'm old and ugly I'll be of no use to anyone. I won't have any choice but to go back to the forest and become a witch or something."

The prince was scowling now.

"You mean you still haven't forgotten about that damned forest? Think of your social position."

"Forgive me. I thought I'd forgotten about it, but on lonely nights like last night it all comes back to me. My mother is a fearsome old witch, but she doted on me when I was growing up. And I know that even when no one wants me any longer, my mother back in the forest will always be willing to hold me in her arms, like she did when I was a little girl."

"But you have me!" said the prince, exasperated.

"No. You too will change. You've treated me nicely, yes, but only because you find me curious and amusing. It's made me feel so lonely, somehow. If I have a baby now, it'll be a new curiosity for you, and you'll forget all about me. I'm really just a foolish and useless person."

"You simply don't realize how beautiful you are." The prince had thrust out his lips in a pout and seemed to moan the words. "You're saying such ridiculous things. Today's question is really dumb."

"You don't understand at all. You don't know how I've been suffering lately. I'm a savage child with the blood of a witch in my veins. How I despise this baby that's going to be born! I wish I could kill it." Rapunzel's voice was trembling. She bit her lower lip.

The prince shuddered. For all his blustering, he was in fact a rather faint-hearted person, and it occurred to him that a woman like Rapunzel might actually go so far as to kill her own child. Women like this, who live by their instincts and don't know how to resign themselves to fate, are always catalysts for tragedy.

The elder daughter had written all this fluidly and unhesitatingly, with an air of absolute self-confidence, and having come this far she quietly laid down her pen. She reread the piece from the beginning, blushing at certain passages and twisting her mouth in a wry smile. There were some rather suggestive scenes here and there, and the poison-tongued second son would probably laugh with scorn when he read it, but there was nothing to be done about that. It seemed to her that she'd set down her own feelings in an honest, straightforward manner, and it made her sad to think how that honesty might be received. On the other hand, she also felt a certain sense of pride: Only she, of all the brothers and sisters, was really capable of expressing the delicacy of a woman's feelings.

There was no heat in her study, and now, suddenly, she became aware of this and shivered: "Brrr . . . I'm *freezing.*" Hunching her shoulders, she stood up clutching the manuscript and hurried out into the hallway, where she nearly collided with her youngest brother. He was standing outside her door looking perturbed and worried.

"Sorry!" he said. "I'm so sorry!"

"Kazu, you've been spying on me."

"No, no, nothing like that!" The accusation flustered him even more, and his face turned bright red.

"I know—you're concerned about whether I was able to continue the story in a satisfactory way. Is that it?"

"Exactly," he confessed in a small voice, then began to berate himself. "Mine wasn't any good, was it? I'm just no good at this."

"That's not true. This time you did very well indeed."

"You really think so?" His small eyes lit up with joy. "Did you do a good job following up on it? Did you do right by Rapunzel?"

"I dare say I did."

"Thank you!" The youngest son pressed his palms together and bowed his head. "Oh, thank you!"

— IV —

The third day.

On New Year's Day, the second son had come to my house on the outskirts of the city and denounced modern Japanese novels one after another, working himself into quite a state of excitement until, at about sunset, he'd muttered, "Uh-oh. I think I'm running a temperature," and hurried home. Sure enough, he developed a mild fever that night. The next day he'd spent in and out of bed, and today, having still not fully recovered, he lay gloomily in his futon, resting his heavy head. That's what happens when you criticize other people's work—you're likely to make yourself ill.

"How are you feeling?" the mother said as she entered her sick child's room. She sat beside his pillow, put her hand to his forehead, and began to scold him at some length.

"Still a bit of a fever. You've got to be more careful. Yesterday you were up and down all day, neglecting your health, eating rice cake and drinking spiced saké . . . You mustn't overextend yourself like that. The best thing for a fever is to lie quietly in bed. It won't do for a person with such a weak constitution to be so strong-headed."

The second son was in low spirits. He offered no retort but merely listened to his mother's complaints with a lopsided smile on his face. Of all the brothers and sisters he was the most objective realist, and the owner of a bitingly caustic tongue, yet toward his mother he was, for some reason, as pliant and submissive as a creeping vine. He was incapable of being high-handed in her presence. It may be that deep in his heart he felt guilty about constantly falling ill and being such a burden to her.

"I want you to stay in bed the entire day today. You mustn't be getting up and wandering all about. You can eat your meals here. I've prepared some rice gruel, and Sato [the maid] is bringing some up for you."

"Mother, I have a favor to ask." He spoke in a weak, defensive tone. "It's my turn today. Is it all right if I write my part?

"What?" His mother looked at him blankly. "What *ever* are you talking about?"

"You know. The chain story. We've started another one. I was bored yesterday, so I talked Hatsué [the elder sister] into showing me the manuscript. I thought about it all night last night, about how to continue. It's going to be kind of difficult this time."

"Absolutely not. I won't hear of it," the mother said, smiling. "Besides, not even great writers can come up with good ideas when they're suffering from a cold. Why don't you let your big brother handle it?"

"Forget that. He won't do at all. He doesn't have any talent. Everything he writes ends up sounding like a speech."

"What a thing to say! Your elder brother always writes the most splendid, manly prose. I, for one, like his pieces best."

"You don't understand these things, Mother. You just don't understand. I have to write the next part, no matter what. I'm the only one who can do it. Please? You'll let me write it, won't you?"

177

"I'm sorry. You've got to stay in bed all day today. Ask your brother to take your turn. You can write your part tomorrow or the next day, when you've got your strength back."

"No I can't. You don't understand. You think it's just some silly little game." He gave an exaggerated sigh of despair and pulled the quilt up over his head.

His mother smiled. "I see. I've hurt your feelings, haven't I? Well, then, why don't we do this: You lie there in bed and dictate to me at your leisure. I'll write it all down just as you tell me. All right? Let's do it that way. Last spring, when you were in bed with a fever, didn't I write out that difficult report of yours for school, just as you dictated it? I did a surprisingly good job that time, didn't I?"

The patient simply lay there with the quilt pulled up over his head and made no reply, leaving the mother somewhat nonplussed. It was at this juncture that the maid, Sato, entered the room carrying a breakfast tray. Sato, who was from a fishing village in the countryside, had worked for the Irie family since she was twelve, and, having lived in the house for four years now, had thoroughly assimilated the family's romantic spirit. She borrowed ladies' magazines from the daughters and read them in her free time, being a particular fan of the old "vendetta tales" they often featured. She was also thoroughly taken with the maxim "Chastity at all costs," and was quietly, fiercely determined to put her life on the line to protect her virtue, should it ever come to that. Hidden in her wicker trunk was a silver paper knife the elder daughter had given her. She thought of it as a dagger, to be used on herself if worst came to worst. She had a darkish complexion but nicely drawn, dainty features, and her clothing was always immaculate. She was slightly lame in her left leg, which tended to drag somewhat when she walked, but in a way this limp of hers was actually rather becoming. She revered the members of the Irie family almost as if they were gods. To her, the grandfather's silver-coin medal seemed an honor of such magnitude that it made her dizzy just to think of it. She firmly believed the elder daughter to be the greatest scholar on earth and the younger daughter the most beautiful woman. But the second son she loved more than life itself. What a thrill it would be to set out with such a handsome young master on a journey to seek revenge! How drab the world was now that people never carried out vendettas, as they had in the past! Such were the idiotic thoughts that often occurred to her.

Sato deferentially set the tray next to the second son's pillow, casting a forlorn glance at the quilt, which was still pulled up over his head. The mother merely looked on, smiling quietly. Sato sat there waiting in silence for some time, but when nothing happened, she turned to the mother and timidly, fearfully asked: "Is it very serious?"

"Well, it's hard to say." The mother was still smiling.

Suddenly the second son threw back his quilt, rolled onto his stomach, pulled the tray over, grabbed the chopsticks, and began to devour the food. Sato was startled but quickly regained her composure and waited on him, relieved to see him exhibiting such vitality. The second son didn't say a word, but it was clear that his appetite was healthy enough: he slurped up his rice gruel at a furious pace and ferociously stuffed his cheeks with pickled plums. Then, as he chipped the shell from a softboiled egg, he spoke.

179

"Sato, what do you think? If, for example, you and I were to get married, how do you think you would feel?"

This was truly a bolt from the blue. If Sato was shocked by the question, the mother was ten times more so.

"My! What an absurd . . . If that's your idea of a joke, young man . . . Sato, he's just teasing you, you know. Of all the outrageous . . . It's not the least bit . . . Good heavens!"

"For example, I mean." The second son was coolly indifferent. All he'd been thinking about since he'd burrowed under his quilt was the plot to the story. A recklessly self-indulgent young man, he had no idea how painfully his "example" had pierced Sato's slender breast.

"How would it make you feel? I need to know. It'll help me write. The story's taken a really difficult turn."

"But it's such a ridiculous thing to ask!" the mother protested, though she was already inwardly relieved. "Sato can't answer a question like that. Can you, Sato? Takeshi [the second son] is just babbling nonsense, isn't he?"

"I . . ." Sato was willing to venture a reply to any question whatsoever if it might be of service to the young master. Ignoring the discomfited gaze the mother was now directing toward her, she steeled her resolve, clenched her fists tightly, and said: "I'd take my own life."

"Oh, great." The second son slumped dejectedly. "That's no good at all. I can't kill Rapunzel off. If she dies, that's the end of the story. Forget it. Damn. This is really difficult. What to do?" He was thoroughly intent on the story, and nothing else. Sato's heroic reply hadn't been of any service after all.

Utterly crestfallen, she quietly stacked the dishes, produced an artificial little laugh to hide her embarrassment, picked up the tray, and fled the room. As she shuffled down the hallway, she considered bursting into tears, but since she wasn't particularly sad she instead began to giggle quite uncontrollably.

The mother felt grateful for the ingenuousness of youth, and was also somewhat ashamed of the turbid state of her own heart and the agitation she had felt. She told herself there was no need to worry.

"Well? Just lie back and let it all come out. I'll write it down for you. Have you gathered your thoughts?"

The second son lay supine again, pulled the quilt up to his chest, closed his eyes, and furrowed his brow. He seemed to be in considerable agony. Finally, in an affected, austere tone of voice, he said: "I believe I have, indeed. Well, then. If you will."

The mother stifled a laugh.

The following is the entire text of that day's son-to-mother dictation.

A beautiful baby boy was born. Everyone in the castle was ecstatic. But Rapunzel, after giving birth, grew weaker with each passing day. The best doctors in the land were summoned, but none of them could do anything to keep her condition from worsening. Soon she was so frail that it was clear her life was in danger.

"I told you . . . I told you." Rapunzel lay in bed quietly shedding tears as she chided her husband. "I told you I didn't want to have a baby. I'm the daughter of a witch . . . I can tell, in a vague sort of way, what lies

181

ahead. I had a premonition that something bad would happen if I gave birth to a child. These premonitions of mine always, always come true. I wouldn't mind dying so much, if that would be the end of the curse. But I have a feeling there's more to it than that. If there really is a God, as you taught me, I think I should pray to Him. Someone holds a grudge against us, I'm sure of it—I can feel it. Maybe we were making a terrible mistake from the beginning."

"No. No, that's not true.' The prince paced back and forth beside Rapunzel's bed, denying everything she said, but inwardly torn and tormented. His joy over the birth of his son had lasted but a fleeting moment before Rapunzel's sudden, mysterious decline; now his anxiety was so great that he was unable to sleep nights and spent all his time pacing his lady's sickroom, utterly beside himself. He did, indeed, love Rapunzel. It would be a mistake to assume that he was merely infatuated with her, that he doted on her only because of the beauty of her face and figure, or because she was, for him, an exotic flower from an alien environment whose ignorance of the world stimulated his protective instincts. And to doubt the sincerity of the prince's love on the grounds that it wasn't born of a lofty spiritual bond or a sense of a common ancestry and destiny, would also be a mistake. The prince adored Rapunzel. He was madly in love with her.

He loved her, that's all. Is that not enough? True love is complete in and of itself. And what women really desire, deep down, is precisely that sort of honest, single-minded devotion. It's one thing to speak of a lofty spiritual bond or commitment to a common destiny, but if the two parties don't love each other, it all comes to nothing. Such high-flown words as "spirituality" and "destiny" have no real meaning without love, and are in fact merely used to manage the flood of lovers' feelings and to justify their passionate behavior. For young lovers, there is nothing so repulsive as such misguided attempts to validate their emotions. Particularly unbearable is the hypocritical man's pose of aiding a damsel in distress. If he loves her, why can't he just state it clearly?

The day before yesterday, when I went to visit the house of the writer D., and this subject came up, D. had the gall to call me a "philistine." I know the man well, however, and from what I've seen of his private life, all I can say is that he himself is a calculating schemer who bases all his actions on sheer self-interest. He's a liar. I don't care if he calls me a philistine. He can call me anything he wishes. I like to tell the truth, just as I see it. It's best to do what one likes.

But I digress. I simply cannot imagine a love based merely on concepts like "spirituality" or "understanding." The prince's love was open and direct. His affection for Rapunzel was of the purest sort. He loved her from the bottom of his heart.

"You mustn't say such crazy things. You're not going to die," he told her now, with a censorious pout. "Don't you realize how much I love you?" The prince was an honest person. But honesty, however noble a virtue, was scarcely enough to save Rapunzel now. "You must live!" he cried. "You mustn't die!" There were no other words left for him to say. His voice dropped to a murmur. "I ask for nothing else—only that you live." And just at that moment, a harsh voice whispered in his ear.

"Do you really mean that? You'll be satisfied if she remains alive, no matter what?"

The prince spun around. His hair was standing on end, and he felt as if his entire body had been doused with ice water. It was Rapunzel's mother, the old witch.

"You!" he bellowed. It was not a courageous bellow, however, but one of terror. "What do you want?"

"I came to help my daughter," the old woman said calmly, then bared her teeth in a smile. "I knew what was happening. There's nothing in this world I don't know. I knew all along that you'd brought my daughter to this castle, and how you've loved and cared for her. Mind you, if I had thought for a moment that you were only toying with her affections, I wouldn't have just stood by and watched. But that didn't seem to be the case, so I've remained in the background all this time and let you be. It gives even an old witch like me a little pleasure to know that her daughter is leading a happy life.

"But it's all over now, isn't it? I don't suppose you know this, but when the daughter of a witch is loved by a man and gives birth to a child, only one of two things can happen: either she dies, or she turns into the ugliest woman in the world. Rapunzel doesn't seem to have been fully aware of this, but she must have had some inkling of what would happen. She didn't want to have a baby, did she? The poor thing. What do you intend to do with her now? Let her die? Or do you want her live on, with a face as hideous as mine? A moment ago you said all you wanted was that she live, no matter what. Did you really mean it? I myself was every bit as beautiful as Rapunzel when I was young. Then a hunter fell in love with me and I ended up giving birth. I wanted to live, at any cost, and that's what I told my mother when she revealed the choice I had to make. She cast a spell and saved my life, but it left me with the spectacular face you see before you. Well? What do you say? Just now you said you ask only that she live. You weren't lying, I take it?"

"Let me die," moaned Rapunzel, writhing on her bed. "If I die, everyone else can go on living in peace. O my prince, you've cared for me all this time, and I ask for nothing more. I don't want to live on in wretchedness."

"Let her live!" the prince bellowed—this time with genuine courage. Hot sweat rolled down his agonized forehead. "Rapunzel will never end up with a face like yours, old witch!"

"You don't believe me? Very well. I'll see to it that Rapunzel lives to a ripe old age. But can you promise you'll always love her, no matter how horrible she ends up looking?"

DAZAI OSAMU

— V —

The passage dictated by the second son from his sickbed appeared, for all its brevity, to constitute a rather considerable leap. Confined to bed and with nothing but rice gruel for nourishment, however, even the haughty, impertinent, spoiled child whose habit it is to heap scorn on the entire roster of contemporary Japanese writers was unable to give us more than a glimpse of his singular genius; indeed, he hadn't spewed out so much as a third of what he'd originally planned to say before he succumbed to exhaustion. It seems, regrettably, that not even genius can overcome the debilitating effects of a mild fever. He'd no sooner begun his great leap forward than he was forced to entrust the baton to the following member of the team.

Next up was the younger daughter, an impertinent thing in her own right. Driven by a lust for glory so pronounced that she'd have preferred to give up entirely on any endeavor rather than fail to attain spectacular success, she was, from the moment she awoke on the fourth day, restless and fidgety. When the whole family gathered at the breakfast table, she alone confined herself to a slice of bread and a glass of milk, perhaps sensing that stuffing herself with such common, down-to-earth dishes as miso soup and pickled radishes could only serve to impede her flights of imagination. After finishing breakfast she went into the parlor, where she stood at the piano and began pounding away at the keys. Chopin, Liszt, Mozart, Mendelssohn, Ravel—she played whatever passage came into her head, a hopeless hodgepodge of melodies. This was her way of calling down inspiration from above. She had always been given to overblown histrionics.

186

Inspiration came. With a serene look on her face, she swept out of the parlor, went to the bathroom, removed her stockings, and washed her feet. A strange thing to do, on the face of it. Apparently she thought of this as a way of purifying herself. A perverse sort of baptism. Now, satisfied that she had attended to the purification of both body and soul, she made a leisurely retreat to her study. Once inside, she sat on a chair, looked up, folded her hands, and murmured:

"Amen."

This was nothing if not extraordinary, since the younger daughter was by no means a religious person. She had merely borrowed the word temporarily, thinking it a suitable vehicle for expressing the precious tension she felt at that moment.

Amen. Indeed, the word seemed to soothe her heart. She ceremoniously dropped a stick of the incense Plum Blossom into the brazier at her feet, took a deep breath, and let her eyelids droop dreamily. She felt as if she understood the state of mind of that great woman writer of olden times, Lady Murasaki, and as she recalled the line "In spring, the dawn," she experienced a rapturous sense of peace and clarity. Then, remembering that the words were in fact written by Sei Shonagon, she came back to earth with a thud and hastily reached for a volume on her desk—*Greek Mythology.* A book of pagan myths. This in itself should suffice to demonstrate the spurious nature of that "Amen" of hers. She claimed that this volume was the fountainhead of her imaginative powers, and that she had only to open it whenever the springs of imagination ran dry, and a flood of flowers, forests, fresh-water pools, love, swans, princes, and fairies welled up before her eyes. This

187

claim of hers was best taken with a grain of salt, however. It was difficult to put much faith in anything the younger daughter said or did. Chopin, inspiration, baptism of the feet, "Amen," Plum Blossom, Lady Murasaki, "In spring, the dawn," Greek mythology—there was no connection at all. Utter incoherence. She was in fact devoted to one thing alone—the act of putting on airs.

After riffling through *Greek Mythology*, pausing to gaze at an illustration of a naked Apollo and to smile a thin, spine-chilling smile, she tossed the book aside, opened her desk drawer, extracted a box of chocolates and a tin of hard candies, and, in a hopelessly affected manner, using only her thumb and forefinger and lifting the other three fingers daintily, selected a chocolate, placed it in her mouth, then chewed and swallowed it noisily even as she reached for a hard candy, which she proceeded to crush between her teeth as she reached for another chocolate, and so on, devouring all before her in the manner of a famished ghoul. With this, of course, her efforts to keep her stomach light and airy by breakfasting only on bread and milk came to naught. The younger daughter was by nature a glutton. She'd attempted to appear refined by limiting herself to a light breakfast, but bread and milk were not enough to satisfy her morning appetite—not by a long shot—and once ensconced in her study, away from prying eyes, she had lost no time in letting loose the trencherman inside her. She was a child prone to deceptions of many and various kinds. After gobbling down twenty chocolates and ten hard candies, she assumed a look of childlike innocence and began humming an aria from *La Traviata*. As she hummed, she brushed the dust from her manuscript paper, filled her artist's pen with ink, and began to

write at a leisurely pace, beginning with a critique which
revealed a somewhat objectionable attitude.

"Women who live by their instincts and don't know
how to resign themselves to fate are always catalysts
for tragedy." This pronouncement left us by Mlle.
Hatsué now appears in danger of being contradicted.
Rapunzel, having grown up in the enchanted forest
eating skewered frogs and poison mushrooms and
being hopelessly spoiled by the old witch's blind love
and doting affection, her only playmates the crows
and deer and other beasts of the forest, was a child of
nature, if you will, and one can agree that there was
indeed something instinctive and primitive about her
tastes and sensibilities. Nor is it difficult to imagine
that the exotic impulsiveness of her behavior was precisely what the prince found so maddeningly attractive. But was Rapunzel, in fact, a woman who didn't
know how to resign herself to fate? We can agree that
she was something of a wild woman and lived by her
instincts, but now, with her life hanging by a thread,
Rapunzel appears, does she not, to have resigned herself completely, to have given up the fight? She says
she wants to die. She says it's best for her to die. Are
these not the words of someone who has resigned herself? And yet Mlle. Hatsué informs us that Rapunzel
is a woman who does not know how to resign herself.
Were we to heedlessly contradict this audacious as-
sertion we would surely be scolded, and since we dis-
like being scolded we shall attempt to defend it.

Rapunzel was a woman who did not know how to
resign herself. "Let me die," she says. It's an utterance
that suggests pathos and self-sacrifice, but if one con-

189

siders carefully one realizes that it is in fact a vain and selfish thing to say. Rapunzel was thinking only of her need to be loved by others. As long as one is capable of believing that one is qualified to receive the love of others, one feels that life is worth living, and the world is a wonderful place. But even if one should discover that one no longer has the necessary qualifications to be loved by others, one must continue to live on. Even if one is not "qualified to be loved," one is eternally "qualified to love." To seek only the joy of being adored is to surrender to savagery and ignorance. From the beginning, Rapunzel has thought of nothing but basking in the prince's affection, and has forgotten to love him in return. She has even forgotten to love the child that she herself gave birth to. No—it's worse than that: she actually resents and envies her child. And now that she believes that she herself will no longer warrant the love of others, what is her wish? "Let me die. Please kill me and have done with it." How selfish can a person be? It is her duty to love the prince more. He too, after all, is a lonely child. Imagine how crushed and defeated Rapunzel's death would leave him! Rapunzel must repay him for his love. And for the sake of her son she must want to live; to want, at all costs, to live. To give that child her affection and think only of raising him to be healthy and strong, no matter how much she might suffer in the process—would not that, in fact, be the true humility of one who knows resignation? The woman who honestly resigns herself to the fact that she herself, being ugly, will not appeal to others, yet who resolves to love nonetheless, even if secretly and from afar, the woman who believes that there is no joy so great as giving of herself—that woman is truly a beloved child of God. Though she might be desired by no one on earth, she shall surely be enveloped in the eternal embrace of God's love. Blessed is she . . .

And so on. Having expounded such awesomely laudable sentiments, it remains only for us to confess that they do not by any means reflect our true feelings. We in fact believe that attaining such beauty that everyone we meet falls madly in love with us, is the highest aspiration for any human being, but we do not wish to invite the wrath of Mlle. Hatsué. Mlle. Hatsué happens to be both our elder sister and our French tutor, which means that we must at all times avoid any defiance of her judgments and devote ourselves to following her lead. "Age before beauty," it is said, but let it not go unnoticed that life can be trying for those who find themselves in the latter category.

Because Rapunzel was, as we have determined, an ignorant person who did not know how to resign herself, no sooner had she sensed that she was about to lose what she perceived as her qualification for being loved, than she began to wish for death. She was without hope. Life, for her, could have no meaning without the prince's love. The prince, for his part, was desperate to save her. When one is in agony, one prays to God, but in the mad delirium of despair, one may be willing even to cling to the devil. The prince, at his wits' end, begged the filthy old witch for help, all but clasping his hands together in supplication.

"Please let her live!" he cried, breaking into a clammy sweat as he fell to his knees before the evil-looking one. To save the life of the woman he loved, he thought nothing of casting away every last ounce of pride and self-respect. Our gallant, our naive, our pure-hearted, pitiful prince.

The old woman smiled. "Very well. Rapunzel shall live to a ripe old age. But even if she ends up with a face like mine, you will continue to love her as always, yes?"

The prince wiped the sweat from his forehead with a fevered sweep of his hand.

"I beg of you. I'm in no state even to consider such a question. I want only to see Rapunzel's health restored. Rapunzel is still young. As long as she's young and healthy, she could never be ugly to me. Please hurry. Make Rapunzel well again." The prince's eyes glistened with tears as he pronounced these bold words. Perhaps to let Rapunzel die while she was still beautiful would be the truest expression of his love ... but it was out of the question. A world without Rapunzel would be as black as night. He wanted her to live. To live and to stay beside him forever. He wasn't concerned about her physical appearance. To lose her would be unbearable. If it weren't for the old witch standing there watching, the prince would have lain down beside his wife, clung to her emaciated breast, and cried: "I love you, Rapunzel! O mysterious flower, nymph of the forest, child of the mountain air, promise you'll never leave my side!"

The old witch narrowed her eyes dreamily, gazing with obvious pleasure at the tortured expression on the prince's face. "What a nice boy," she muttered, in her raspy voice. "What a nice, honest boy. Rapunzel, you're a lucky girl."

"No," Rapunzel moaned from her sickbed. "I'm a child of misfortune. I'm the daughter of a witch. When the prince shows me his love, it only makes me all the more aware of my lowly birth. I'm so ashamed . . . I always think of our old home in the forest, and sometimes I even feel my life was easier when I was shut up in the tower, communing with the birds and stars. I don't know how many times I thought of fleeing this castle and returning home. But I couldn't bear to part with the prince. I love him. I would give him my life ten times over if I could. The prince is a kind and gentle person, and I just couldn't bring myself to leave him. That's why I've remained here all this time. I have not been happy. Every day has been hell for me. Oh, Mother! A woman should never take for her husband a man she loves with all her heart. She'll not be the least bit happy. No, Mother, let me die! I'll never leave the prince as long as I live—so let me leave him by ending my life. If I die, the prince and everyone else can find happiness."

"That's just your selfishness speaking." The old woman said this with a snaggle-toothed sneer, but the words reverberated with motherly love. "The prince has promised to care for you no matter how ugly you become. He's mad about you. I must say I'm impressed. The way things stand, if you were to die, why, he might even follow you in death. You wouldn't want that to happen, would you? For the prince's sake, you must regain your strength and see what happens. Let the future take care of itself. Rapunzel, don't you understand? You've given birth to a baby. You're a mother now."

Rapunzel breathed a faint sigh and quietly closed her eyes. The prince, exhausted by his own extreme emotions, now stood frozen in one spot, his face a blank, expressionless mask as, before his eyes and with unimaginable speed, the witch constructed a black magic altar. She dashed out of the room and was no sooner gone than she appeared again, carrying something in her arms, and no sooner had she appeared than she vanished and was back again carrying something else, and so on, until the room was filled with bizarre and wondrous objects. The altar stood upon the four legs of a beast and was covered with a crimson cloth that was made of the dried tongues of five hundred species of snakes and owed its color to the blood that had dripped from those tongues. On top of the altar was an enormous cauldron fashioned from the hide of a black cow, inside of which, though there was no fire, water boiled furiously, all but spilling over the sides. The old witch, her hair in wild disarray, ran round and round the altar, chanting some sort of incantation and tossing rare medicinal herbs and other extraordinary ingredients into the cauldron. Snow that had lain atop a lofty mountain peak since ancient times, frost from bamboo leaves that glittered in the last split second before melting, the shell of a tortoise that had lived ten thousand years, gold dust gathered flake by flake in the moonlight, the scales of a dragon, the eyes of a rat that had never seen sunlight, quicksilver regurgitated by a cuckoo, the glowing tail of a firefly, the blue tongue of a cockatoo, an eternally blooming poppy, the earlobe of an owl, the toenails of a ladybug, the back teeth of a katydid, a plum blossom from the bottom of the sea, and many other precious and all-but-unobtainable objects—one by one she threw them into the boiling mixture, circling the altar some three hundred times before finally coming to a halt. The moment she stopped, the steam that rose from the cauldron began to glow with the seven colors of the rainbow.

"Rapunzel!" the witch shouted in a voice so powerful and commanding that it was scarcely recognizable. "I am about to perform a once-in-a-lifetime feat of sorcery, a tremendously difficult operation. Bear with me!" And with that, she drew a long, narrow dagger, straddled her daughter where she lay, and drove it into her breast. Before the prince even had time to let out a cry of horror, the witch had lifted Rapunzel's wasted body above her head and thrown her into the cauldron—*splash!* A faint cry, like the sob of a seagull, was the only sound that followed the splash; afterward all was silence except for the bubbling of the boiling water and the old witch's muttered incantations.

Overwhelmed by what had just happened, the prince was dumbstruck for some time. Finally, in a voice that was scarcely more than a mumble, he said: "What the hell are you doing? I didn't ask you to kill her. I didn't tell you to boil her in your cauldron. Bring her back. Bring my Rapunzel back to me, you demon!"

This much he said, but he did not have the energy or will to challenge the witch any further. He flung himself on Rapunzel's empty bed and began to sob and whimper like a child.

The old witch paid no attention to him but continued to chant, staring with bloodshot eyes at the boiling water as sweat coursed down her face and neck. Then,

Dazai Osamu

suddenly, she ceased her incantations, and at that very instant the water stopped boiling. The prince, with tears still streaming down his cheeks, lifted his head to peer questioningly at the cauldron.

"Arise, Rapunzel!" the witch called out in a clear, exultant voice. And then, rising from the cauldron, there appeared . . . Rapunzel's face.

— VI —

She was beautiful. Her face fairly shone with radiant beauty.

So wrote the eldest son, bursting with excitement as he continued the story.

The eldest son's fountain pen was remarkable if only for its extraordinary girth. It was about the size of a sausage. Gripping this magnificent instrument tightly in his right hand, he threw out his chest and pressed his lips together in a straight, hard line, maintaining an air of great moment as he drew each character with large, bold strokes, but, sad to say, the eldest son was not blessed with the storytelling talent of his brothers and sisters. They, for their part, often made fun of him for that shortcoming, but this was merely proof of their own insolence and moral lassitude. The eldest son possessed impeccable virtues of his own, and they happened to be attributes that were indispensable to one in his position as eldest. He told no lies. He was an honest man. And he was what one might call, for lack of a better word, sentimental. He was simply not capable of writing something to the effect that Rapunzel had emerged from the cauldron with a face as ugly and fearsome as that of the old witch. He just couldn't do that to poor Rapunzel. Nor, he thought, with something approaching righteous indignation, would it be fair to the prince. It was, therefore, with great fervor that he wrote these lines. "She was beautiful. Her face fairly shone with radiant beauty."

After he'd written that, however, he was stuck. The eldest son had always been too serious, and his powers of imagination were as a consequence severely underdeveloped. It would seem that the more irresponsible and crafty one is, the more likely one is to have a talent for storytelling. The eldest son was a man of irreproachable character. He burned with lofty-minded ideals and a had a deep affection for others that was devoid of any calculating self-interest—attributes that left him out of his element when it came to fabricating tales. He was, to put it more bluntly, a lousy storyteller. Whatever he attempted to write, it quickly began to sound like an academic treatise. This time he seemed in danger of slipping into an oratorical mode, but he was, if nothing else, in absolute earnest. "Her face fairly shone with radiant beauty." After writing this, he solemnly closed his eyes and sat there as if lost in profound meditation. It was some time before he opened his eyes again and continued to write, more slowly this time. The following passage is his contribution. It isn't much in terms of story, but one can detect between the lines the eldest son's sincerity and compassion.

> It was not the face of Rapunzel. Or, rather, it was the face of Rapunzel, but not the same downy-cheeked face she'd had before her illness; not the same sweet face that reminded one of a wild rose (if one may be forgiven the indiscretion of appearing to critique a lady's features). Were we to compare the faintly smiling face of the revived Rapunzel to a flower (impudent as it may be to liken the face of a human being, the crown of creation, to mere flora), perhaps it would have to be a Chinese bellflower. Or perhaps an evening primrose. An autumn flower, in any case. Climbing out of the cauldron, she stepped down from the witch's altar and smiled sadly. Grace—that's the word. She was endowed with a refined, dignified grace

that she had previously lacked, and the prince instinctively gave a short bow to the genteel, queenly figure that stood before him.

"This is very strange," said the old witch. "This isn't what was supposed to happen. I was expecting a girl with a face like a toad to come crawling out of the cauldron. A power greater than my witchcraft must have interfered. I'm defeated. That does it. I've had my fill of witchcraft. I'm going back to the forest to be a normal, boring old woman for the rest of my life. There are things in this world I just don't understand." And with that, she kicked the altar over and fed it to the fire in the hearth. It's said that the exotic contents of the altar burned with a brilliant blue flame for seven days and seven nights. And the witch, true to her word, returned to the forest and quietly passed the remainder of her days as an unexceptional, mild-mannered old hag.

What this means, of course, is that the power of the prince's love had won out over the witch's magic, and, in this writer's opinion, it was from this point on that the prince and Rapunzel's real life together as a married couple finally began. It might not be going too far to say that the prince's attachment to Rapunzel had until now been based on little more than physical attraction. This, perhaps, cannot be helped for one who is still in his youth. But physical attraction inevitably wanes, and a crisis inevitably ensues. The young couple's love had suffered a setback due primarily to Rapunzel's pregnancy and the birth of their child, and this, no doubt, was God's way of testing their love. But the prince's ingenuous, fervent prayers had been heard, and God, in his benevolence and mercy, saw to it that Rapunzel was resurrected as a woman of refined, lofty spiritual qualities that outshone even her astounding physical beauty. Thus it was that the prince instinctively bowed to his wife upon beholding her.

There it is, right there. That bow is where their new married life begins. A life based upon mutual respect. Without mutual respect, there can be no true nuptial bond. Rapunzel was no longer a savage child. Nor was she anyone's plaything. With a smile of deep sorrow, resignation, and mercy on her lips, she stood as serenely composed as a natural-born queen. The prince, too, merely by returning that smile, was imbued with a profound and mellow sense of well-being. A husband and wife must remarry any number of times in their lives. In order to discover each other's true worth, they must forge ahead together, overcoming crisis after crisis, never separating but renewing their vows again and again. It may be that five years from now, or ten years, the prince and Rapunzel will find themselves in the position of having, once again, to reaffirm their union, but in this writer's opinion, they are not likely ever to lose the intense trust and respect that they have now acquired for each other, and we are probably justified in offering, at this point, three rousing cheers for the young couple.

The eldest son had written this with such gravity and force of conviction that now not even he knew what he was trying to say, and he grew a bit disconcerted. He could see he'd done nothing to advance the story, and even wondered if he hadn't managed to destroy it entirely. He sat clutching his fat fountain pen with a hopelessly glum look on his face until, desperate, he stood up and began taking books from his shelves and leafing through them. Finally he found something suitable. It was from the New Testament, the first letter of Paul to Timothy. He nodded to himself, convinced he'd found just the thing with which to conclude the story of Rapunzel, and, with an air of tremendous solemnity, began copying down the words.

"I desire then that in every place the men should pray, lifting holy hands without anger or quarreling; also that women should adorn themselves modestly and sensibly in seemly apparel, not with braided hair or gold or pearls or costly attire but by good deeds, as befits women who profess religion. Let a woman learn in silence with all submissiveness. I permit no woman to teach or to have authority over men; she is to keep silent. For Adam was formed first, then Eve; and Adam was not deceived, but the woman was deceived and became a transgressor. Yet woman will be saved through bearing children, if she continues in faith and love and holiness, with modesty."

That should wrap it up nicely, the eldest son thought, smiling to himself. It would also serve as a good admonition for the younger brothers and sisters. If it hadn't been for this passage from Paul, his argument would have seemed incoherent, treacly, and conventional to a degree, and might even have invited the scornful laughter of the younger siblings. It had been a close call, and he gave thanks to Paul for helping him escape disaster. The eldest son never forgot to include a moral for the others. The moral, in fact, was his main concern, which was why he always grew overly serious, preventing the story from proceeding smoothly and turning it into a sermon. Being the eldest, he felt he had to be sober-minded at all times, and his sense of responsibility would not allow him to participate in the younger brothers and sisters' nonsensical jesting.

At any rate, with this more or less superfluous lecture on morality, the eldest son had somehow managed to bring the story to a close within the appointed time. Today was the fifth day of the new year. The second son had recovered from his cold. It was shortly after noon when the eldest left his study in high spirits and walked about the house informing the others that the story was complete and instructing them to gather in the drawing room. The grandfather joined them, grinning, and in a while the grandmother also suffered herself to be dragged into the room by the youngest son. The mother and Sato busied themselves heating up the brazier, preparing tea, serving confections, laying out sandwiches for lunch, and fetching a bottle of whiskey for the grandfather.

First the youngest son read his passage haltingly, embarrassed and distracted by the grandmother's ejaculations of approval each time he paused for breath. In the confusion of the moment, the grandfather drew the whiskey bottle to his side, uncapped it, and began helping himself quite freely to the contents. The eldest son quietly whispered: "Grandfather, aren't you overdoing it a bit?" But the grandfather replied in an even quieter whisper: "Any connoisseur knows you've got to be drunk to really enjoy a good romance."

The youngest son, the elder daughter, the second son, and the younger daughter all read their contributions in turn, making use of a rich variety of dramatic vocal techniques, and then the eldest brother read his part in the sorrowful screech of someone delivering a fiery patriotic oration. The second son tried not to laugh but finally, unable to contain himself any longer, dashed out into the hall. The younger daughter displayed her absolute scorn for the eldest son's literary talent by sarcastically feigning wide-eyed admiration and even applauding from time to time. She was, as has been noted, an impertinent thing.

By the time all of them had finished reading, the grandfather was more than a little drunk. "Bravo! Bravo! Very well done, all of you. The part by Rumi [the younger daughter] was especially good," he said, singling out his favorite grandchild as usual. "However," he continued, opening his bleary eyes wide and launching into an unexpected criticism. "It's too bad you all concentrated on Rapunzel and the prince and scarcely touched upon the king and queen. Hatsué wrote a little bit about them, as I recall, but that wasn't nearly enough. The only reason the prince and Rapunzel were able to get married in the first place, and the only reason they managed to live happily ever after, was because of the king and queen's generosity. If they had been less tolerant and understanding, no matter how deeply Rapunzel and the prince loved each other, it would have all been for nothing. The story's incomplete if you ignore the magnanimity of the king and queen. You kids are young yet. You concentrate only on the prince and Rapunzel's love and don't notice the forces behind the scenes that make it all possible. You've still got a lot to learn. Look at Victor Hugo, for example. I've been a fan of Hugo's works for years, ever since Shinnosuke, your father, recommended them to me. Now there's an author who overlooks nothing. Old Victor Hugo would never—"

His voice had risen to a near shout when his wife cut him off.

"What sort of nonsense are you babbling?" she snapped. "Just when the children are enjoying themselves!"

The grandfather was not only sharply reprimanded but relieved of his whiskey bottle. Though his critique may have had its merits, the manner in which he'd presented it had been decidedly less than tactful, and no one rose to support him. They all looked on in stony silence. When a dejected shadow fell over the old man's face, however, the mother, who couldn't bear to see him like that, quietly handed him the famous silver-coin medal. She'd been awarded the medal on New Year's Eve, when she'd paid off a certain small debt the grandfather had secretly incurred.

"Grandfather's going to bestow the medal on the person who did the best job," she announced, smiling, to the children.

This, obviously, was a means by which she hoped to perk up the old man's spirits, but he, with an untypically somber expression on his face, shook his head and said: "No. No, I'm going to give it to you, Miyo [the mother]. It's yours permanently now. Promise you'll always take good care of these fine grandchildren of mine."

The brothers and sisters were all quite moved. It seemed to them a very special honor indeed.

Made in United States
Orlando, FL
22 March 2023

31315070R00136